BREAK
and
ENTER

^A Chloe & Levesque
MYSTERY

BOOK 4

Norah McClintock

The Chloe and Levesque Series

Over the Edge
Double Cross
Scared to Death
Break and Enter

BREAK and ENTER

^A Chloe & Levesque
MYSTERY

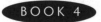
BOOK 4

Norah McClintock

Kane Miller
A DIVISION OF EDC PUBLISHING

First American Edition 2011
Kane Miller, A Division of EDC Publishing

Copyright © 2001 by Norah McClintock.
First published by Scholastic Canada Ltd.

Library of Congress Control Number: 2010933236

Printed and bound in the United States of America
1 2 3 4 5 6 7 8 9 10
ISBN: 978-1-61067-005-0

BREAK and ENTER

A Chloe & Levesque

MYSTERY

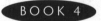
BOOK 4

Norah McClintock

Kane Miller
A DIVISION OF EDC PUBLISHING

First American Edition 2011
Kane Miller, A Division of EDC Publishing

For information contact:
Kane Miller, A Division of EDC Publishing
PO Box 470663
Tulsa, OK 74147-0663
www.kanemiller.com
www.edcpub.com

Library of Congress Control Number: 2010933236

Printed and bound in the United States of America
1 2 3 4 5 6 7 8 9 10
ISBN: 978-1-61067-005-0

To George, Bob, Tom, Roy and Jeff —
but mostly to George

Chapter 1

It started in Mr. Lawry's history class. Mr. Lawry wasn't standing at the front of the class at the time. He wouldn't be standing there for another six to eight weeks, which was part of the problem. His car had been sideswiped by some college kids heading home after a little too much partying in Elder Bay. The college kids walked away without a scratch, although I heard that the front end of their Subaru looked like a squeezed-in accordion. Mr. Lawry didn't walk away at all. He ended up in the hospital with one broken hip and one broken leg. Replacing him at East Hastings Regional High was a newly graduated keener named Mr. Green.

Mr. Green looked a maximum of two years older than the kids he was supposed to be teaching. He acted like a middle-aged prison guard. He had zero sense of humor, so it wouldn't surprise me if he ended up as a vice-principal at some point in his career. He'd be good at it too, because he was incapable of looking at both sides of any issue — or even, as far as I could tell, of acknowledging that there was any side other than his own.

Before his unfortunate accident, Mr. Lawry had scheduled a test. On his third day at East Hastings Regional, Mr. Green gave us the test. The topic? Changes in Lower Canada following the victory of the British over the French on the Plains of Abraham. I knew the subject backward and forward. I'd been born and raised in Quebec. They serve you that stuff in kindergarten with your glass of milk and carrot sticks. My point being, I barely needed to study, let alone resort to dishonesty, to pass the test.

So there I was, sitting in my usual place, third row from the door, fifth seat from the front of the class, writing test answers onto the test answer paper. On my left was Dean Abbott, a big guy, a year older than almost everyone else in the class, and no Einstein. Behind him were Rick Antonio and Brad Hudson, who, as athletes, possessed a keen knowledge of sports and no particular interest in history. On my right was Davis Kaye, the new kid, dressed in his hip Toronto black, a pair of sunglasses hooked on the neck of his T-shirt. Directly in front of me sat Daria Dattillo. She'd swapped seats with Vanessa Sutherland right after Christmas. I'm sure she did it because it was the one place in the room where she would never have to make eye contact with me. Daria didn't like me much, but that's another story. Directly behind me was Julie March. She didn't like history. She also didn't like French, math, science or English. A row over from her, head down, scribbling away madly (always scribbling away madly when she wasn't waving her hand in the air in response to a question), was Sarah Moran, East Hastings Regional's honor roll queen — until the end of last term when I displaced her. This seemed to be eating at Sarah, but I didn't care.

Suddenly, marching down the aisle toward me was Mr. Green. He stopped beside my desk, but I didn't look up. Why should I? I was busy acing my test.

"Problem, Mr. Kaye?" Mr. Green said, apparently to Davis.

Davis had been sitting next to me in history for the six weeks he had lived in East Hastings. He never tired of telling anyone who would listen — and plenty of people who weren't even remotely interested in listening — how much better and more interesting life was in Toronto and how much cooler and smarter he was than any of us. His proximity had engendered in me the sincere hope that Davis not only had a problem, but that he had a whole sack full of them.

Davis didn't answer Mr. Green. At least, he didn't answer in words. I found out later, from people who had been happy to have something distract them from the test, that Davis had responded by nodding in my direction. Specifically, in the direction of the floor under my desk. But I didn't know that at the time. All I knew was that Mr. Green was standing beside me, and that maybe he was looking at Davis and maybe he was looking at me. I didn't care. I was into the Zen of the test. I knew the answers to every single question on that test page. And those answers were flowing out of my fingertips and through my pen onto the paper. I knew this stuff cold. If Mr. Green wanted to observe the miracle of my brilliance at work, hey, that was okay with me.

Then Mr. Green ducked down beside me. That got my attention. I hadn't heard him drop anything, so what was he doing? I looked up from my test just as he was straightening again. He was holding a piece of paper in his hand. He peered at it. He looked down at me. Then he snatched the answer paper off my desk and peered at that. His normally serious expression turned downright grim.

"Hey!" I said, when he grabbed my paper. Then I made what turned out to be my first mistake of the day. I gave in to the urge to seize the paper from him.

The first splotches appeared just above his shirt collar.

Besides having the personality of a parking enforcement officer, Mr. Green was an explosive blusher. Whenever he got emotional, he got splotchy. It didn't seem to matter whether the emotion was annoyance or anger or embarrassment, a little patch of red would appear on his neck, as if he'd been dabbed by a paintbrush. A second splotch would follow the first, a little higher up on his neck. Then another and another. They reminded me of fat raindrops hitting the pavement at the beginning of a storm, *splat, splat, splat*, until the whole pavement was wet. Or, in Mr. Green's case, until his whole face was crimson. It was a trait that could be useful — to his enemies. You could see how well your zingers were hitting home by how fast and how far the splotches spread. I would have loved to play poker with Mr. Green — for money, not matchsticks.

"You will report to the office this minute," he said to me.

"What for?" That was mistake number two. Apparently teachers — well, *some* teachers — don't like students talking back to them. Although, technically, I wasn't talking, I was asking a question.

He held up the paper that he had retrieved from the floor. It took a moment for me to focus. When I did, I saw that it was covered with notes — notes on the consequences of the French defeat on the Plains of Abraham. The notes were written in purple ink. I always write in purple ink. Hey —

"That isn't mine, if that's what you think," I said.

"To the office," he said. Actually, he commanded. "Wait for me there."

I couldn't believe it. He thought I was cheating.

"I could pass this test blindfolded," I said.

"Office!" he said. The splotches had passed chin level and were advancing on his cheeks.

"That isn't mine," I said again. I glanced around the class. Everyone was staring at me. A few —

Rick Antonio, Brad Hudson and Sarah Moran among them — were smiling.

"If I have to tell you one more time — "

"Fine," I said. "I'll go."

* * *

Ms. Jeffries, the principal of East Hastings Regional High, peered over the tops of her reading glasses at me when I entered the office.

"Good morning, Chloe," she said. "To what do we owe the pleasure of this visit?"

"Mr. Green sent me."

She waited. When I didn't elaborate, she said, "And may I ask why?"

I opened my mouth to tell her, then decided to let her hear it directly from Mr. Green. "He told me to wait here for him," I said.

I didn't have to wait long. Ten minutes after I took a seat on the bench, the bell rang. A couple of minutes after that, Mr. Green strode into the office, carrying my test and the sheet of paper he had found under my desk.

"I caught this girl cheating," he said.

Ms. Jeffries looked at me in surprise.

"Perhaps you should both come into my office," she said.

We followed her behind the counter and into the largest of the three small offices that ran down the corridor alongside the main office. She sat at her desk and waved us into a couple of chairs facing her.

"Now then," she said, "what's this all about?" She

was looking at me.

"I don't know," I said. "I was writing my history test and all of a sudden Mr. Green grabbed it out of my hand and told me to come down here."

Ms. Jeffries shifted her attention to Mr. Green.

"I found this under her desk," he said. He handed her the first sheet of paper. "See for yourself. These are definitely crib notes and this is definitely her handwriting." He handed her the second sheet, my test answers.

Ms. Jeffries put on her reading glasses again and examined both papers. Her usually smiling face turned serious.

"Can you explain this, Chloe?"

Her solemn tone startled me. She pushed the papers across the desk toward me. I looked more closely at the crib sheet. Even I couldn't hide my shock.

"This isn't mine," I said, but I felt like a character in one of those cheesy science fiction movies who has just been confronted with the impossible — a living, breathing, three-eyed creature from outer space. The crib notes weren't just written in purple ink. They were written in handwriting that looked an awful lot like my own.

"I promise these aren't mine, Ms. Jeffries," I said. "You know me." Okay, so she'd only known me for a grand total of seven months — hardly a lifetime. "I don't need to cheat in history. It's one of my best subjects."

"Maybe it's one of your best subjects because of

the way you approach your tests," Mr. Green suggested.

"I'd like to hear your explanation for this, Chloe," Ms. Jeffries said.

"I don't have an explanation. That isn't my paper."

Ms. Jeffries sighed and leaned back in her chair. "If you were cheating, that's very serious," she said. She sounded confused by what I had supposedly done, which I guess should have been comforting. Unlike Mr. Green, she wasn't assuming that cheating was a way of life with me. But I wasn't comforted. I was mad.

"That paper is *not* mine," I said again. Maybe I said it a little too loudly. Maybe it sounded like I was shouting.

"Anyone caught cheating gets an automatic zero," Mr. Green said. "Those are the rules." He was exactly the kind of person who read and probably memorized rule books.

"Give me a break — "

Ms. Jeffries looked down at the two papers. She studied first one, then the other. When she looked up at me, I read disappointment in her eyes. "I don't understand why you would do something like this, Chloe, but I'm afraid I have to agree with Mr. Green," she said. "Zero on the test and one week's detention."

"One week?" That voice of disbelief was Mr. Green's, not mine. "For something this serious — "

Ms. Jeffries silenced him with a stern look.

"You may go," she said to me.

Thanks a million.

* * *

"Is it true?" Ross asked, as he slipped into the seat beside me in the cafeteria. Ross Jenkins is editor of the school newspaper and supposedly a friend of mine. But what kind of friend would ask a question like that? I looked up at him for a moment, then stuck my nose back in my book.

"I heard the crib sheet was in your handwriting," he said.

I turned the page and kept reading.

"Was it?" he said.

He was starting to make me angry.

"Let me get this straight," I said. "You're asking me if it's true that I was cheating on a history test, is that it? Is that what you want to know?"

To his credit, he looked embarrassed. "Don't get me wrong," he said. "I know you didn't do it."

"Then why are you asking?"

"Everyone says the crib sheet was in your handwriting."

"And how exactly does *everyone* know that?" I asked. "*Everyone* didn't see it."

"Davis saw it. So did Julie March."

"Obviously they've been spreading the word," I said. Friends! Okay, so technically neither Davis nor Julie were friends of mine. But what were they doing gossiping about me? Well, okay, so it made a good story. And maybe I'd do the same thing myself if someone I knew had been caught cheating. There was just one small problem. I hadn't been cheating.

"So you're saying it wasn't your handwriting?" Ross said.

I had expected better from him. When I didn't get it, I closed my book, stood up and marched out of the cafeteria.

* * *

I finished the rest of the school day, served my detention, and headed home an hour later than usual. I was trudging along Centre Street near where it joined Cedar Road, which is the road I live on, when a police squad car pulled up beside me. Levesque was behind the wheel. That's Louis Levesque, my stepfather and East Hastings's chief of police. I climbed in.

"Tough day?" he asked, after a few moments of silence.

"Yeah."

"Want to tell me about it?"

"No."

Silence. Merciful silence, I thought. I should have known better. I should have realized that those few quiet moments were intended to give me a chance to rethink my answer — the theory being that a large percentage of wrongdoers are eager to confess their crimes and get them off their chest. A good cop gives them that chance. If they don't take it, then the cop moves into interrogation mode.

"I got a call from Alice Jeffries this afternoon," he said.

If I had bet on the next question he was going to ask, I would have won big.

"You want to tell me what happened?" he said. That was every police officer's number one favorite question. Sometimes I think they tattoo it on recruits' butts at police college.

"What for? If you talked to Ms. Jeffries, you already know what happened."

We were about halfway up Cedar Road, but instead of driving on, Levesque pulled over to the side of the road.

"Correct me if I'm wrong," he said, "but you're an A-student in history."

I didn't say anything. There was nothing to correct.

"Which is why it strikes me as unlikely that you would cheat," he said.

"Thank you." If I sounded sarcastic, blame it on the word *unlikely*. What was wrong with the word *impossible*?

"Got any enemies?" he said.

I thought he was kidding.

"Or maybe a doppelganger," he said. I saw the hint of a smile beneath his bushy moustache.

"Right," I said. "Just what I need, an evil twin sister."

"Just what the world needs," he said. Then he got serious again. "Alice said she had no choice but to give you a zero on the test. I got the impression she felt bad about it."

"She was disappointed in me, right? Just like you are."

He fixed me with his coal-colored eyes. When he looked at me like that, I always felt sorry for the bad guys he had grilled over the years. They'd never had a chance.

"I'm not disappointed," he said, "because there's nothing to be disappointed about. You're not a cheater."

Okay. That sounded like he believed I was innocent.

"And, believe me," he said, "if I ever found out you were cheating, my disappointment wouldn't be the main thing you'd have to worry about."

"Everyone thinks I did it," I said.

"Everyone?"

"Well, a lot of people."

"Not the people who know you," he said.

Read: not the important people. Well, not most of the important people. I wasn't so sure about Ross.

"It sure looked like my handwriting," I said. That was the thing that had been bothering me the most.

He put the car back into gear and pulled out onto Cedar Road again.

"If you didn't write those notes and if you didn't drop them under your desk," he said, "then you have to wonder, who did?"

Chapter 2

On the plus side, I thought, as I reached for my morning cup of coffee, hump day was behind me. If Wednesday was the big bulge in the week, then Thursday was the beginning of the slow slide toward the weekend. Hallelujah! On the minus side, I had history today. I had asked almost everyone in my history class, but I hadn't gotten an inch closer to discovering how that crib sheet had ended up under my desk. Nobody, it seemed, knew anything. Nobody had seen anything. And I had the third of my five detentions to look forward to at the end of the day. If Mr. Green's track record was anything to go by, he would drop by to make sure I was serving it. I decided to send Mr. Lawry a get-well-soon card.

I was at the kitchen table, gulping coffee and stuffing notebooks and textbooks into my back-pack, when a big bowl of gluey-looking glop appeared in front of me. Shendor, our golden retriever, sniffed at it, then turned and skulked out of the room. I used to think she would eat anything, but even she drew the line at oatmeal.

"What is this?" I asked Levesque.

He shook his head. "And you on the honor roll," he said.

Très amusant. "Let me rephrase," I said. *"Why* is this?"

"It'll get your day off to a good start."

Just then Phoebe breezed into the kitchen. Phoebe is my kid sister. Among her more irritating qualities is her first-thing-in-the-morning perkiness. People who are as cheerful as Phoebe in the early morning should be sentenced to a lifetime of daily six a.m. cheerleader practice to soak up their excess rah-rah attitude and spare the rest of us from their Disney-esque enthusiasm.

"Oooh! Oatmeal!" she said, as if the pot Levesque was holding were full of thousand-dollar bills. "How come?"

Levesque glopped a pile of beige sludge into a bowl for her.

"It's good for you," he said.

"You sound like that sour old man on TV," I said. I watched Phoebe pour milk over her cereal and sprinkle it with brown sugar, which she tried to pass to me.

"No, thanks," I said. I don't like oatmeal. I don't like anything but an infusion of coffee first thing in the morning, although I usually take a piece of fruit or a bagel and cheese with me on the walk to school. By the time I'm halfway there, my stomach generally wakes up.

"You should at least try it," Levesque said to me.

"This is about that book Mom was reading, right?" I said.

"What book?" Mr. Poker-Face was looking a little uncomfortable now. Good.

"You know, the one about how to live healthy when you're over the hill."

Phoebe giggled.

"Are you saying your mother is over the hill?" Levesque asked. Nice dodge.

"She has two kids in high school and one in college." My sister Brynn had stayed in Montreal to attend Dawson College. Mom was there for a couple of weeks, visiting her. "That definitely makes her older than the average spring chicken," I said. "And you're even older than her, right?"

"Eat your oatmeal," he said. Phoebe had already eaten most of hers.

"Where's yours?" I asked Levesque.

He glopped more oatmeal into a bowl, presumably for himself. The phone rang. Levesque got to it before either Phoebe or I could stand up. If you ask me, he seemed a little too eager.

"When?" he said into the phone. Then, "Where?" Two words that meant police business. "Okay. I'll be right there."

"Rushing off without your oatmeal?" I said, as he hung up.

To my surprise, he carried his bowl to the table, sat down, and poured some milk into it.

"Wasn't that Steve on the phone?" I asked. Steve Denby worked with Levesque.

"It was."

"You said you'd be right there."

He shrugged. "There's been a break-in at one of the cottages up near the park," he said. "Whoever did it is long gone, so there's no need to skip a good breakfast before heading out." With that, he looked pointedly at my own rapidly cooling bowl of oatmeal.

"Good breakfast?" I said, my gaze darting around the kitchen. "Where?"

* * *

Rick Antonio was perched on the hood of his car, an old black Chevette of which he was far too proud. I mean, come on, a Chevette? It was parked in the corner of the school lot. When I saw him, I considered a detour. Rick didn't like me and I didn't like him, ever since I had temporarily lost my mind a few weeks back and had said yes when he asked me to go to a concert with him in Morrisville. The concert was mediocre. The drive back to East Hastings was excruciating — forty-five minutes of head-banger music and nonstop jock talk. When he tried to park and "have a little fun" — his words, not mine — we got into a fight. I made him take me home. For the first couple of days after that, Rick ignored me at school. Then he started riding me every chance he got, calling me Ice Princess and chucking crumpled up pieces of paper at the back of my head in history class. Once I walked into the classroom and saw *For a good time, DON'T call Chloe* scrawled on the blackboard. I can't prove he wrote it, but I would have been willing to put big bucks on it.

I glanced at him now. He had seen me and was watching me, so I kept going, heading right toward him. He grinned.

"Hey, sweetheart," he said.

I ignored him.

He slid down off the hood and blocked my path.

"Hey, honey, I'm talking to you," he said.

"Oh," I said. "I didn't realize. My name isn't sweetheart or honey."

"Right," he said, still smiling. "I forgot. There's nothing sweet about you. Guess maybe if I'd said Ice Princess I would have gotten a reaction."

He might even have gotten a slap.

"What do you want, Rick?"

"Just trying to be friendly," he said. "Some people make an effort, you know."

I started to move past him.

"Hey," he said. I knew there had to be more. With a sigh, I turned to face him. "You know what they say," he said. "Cheaters never prosper."

"Glad to see you were paying attention back there in kindergarten, Rick," I said. "Got any other gems of wisdom you want to pass along?"

He shook his head and let out a long, noisy sigh. "Little Miss Perfect," he said. "And it turned out she cheated her way to an A."

I ignored the comment and walked into the school. He was such an idiot. But I couldn't help wondering — was this idiot smart enough to have landed me in trouble in the first place? And if he was, how could I find out?

* * *

"Pick one of the topics on the sheet," Mr. Green said. "I want a fifteen-hundred-word essay from each of you."

There was a moment of silence as everyone did the math, then a collective groan went up. Fifteen hundred words translated into six pages, typed, double-spaced. Ten or twelve pages if you wrote it out by hand. Mr. Lawry used to limit us to three or four pages. He always said that was plenty to demonstrate knowledge of a subject. That was one more difference between Mr. Lawry and Mr. Green.

"I expect your work to be original," Mr. Green said. "No copying from other books. No borrowing old term papers. No downloading essays from the Internet." He looked directly at me. "Do I make myself clear, Chloe?"

Whoa! He was warning me, specifically. Which meant that he thought I needed special warning.

"You're making yourself perfectly clear, Mr. Green," I said.

He liked that. He smiled around the class.

"Mr. Green?" I said.

He turned back to me.

"I'm just wondering, is there some special reason that you directed that comment at me?"

He didn't say anything.

"Because it sounds like you're warning *me* not to

plagiarize. I think that's unfair."

By this time everyone in the class was staring at me — well, everyone except Daria Dattillo, who sat directly in front of me and was making a career out of pretending I didn't exist. I felt like telling Mr. Green that if anyone needed a warning against plagiarism, it was Daria. In fact, plagiarism was the whole reason she hated me. I had caught her at it. I had exposed her and she had never forgiven me.

"I'm warning *everyone* not to plagiarize," Mr. Green said. "That includes you."

I had to hand it to him, nice recovery. I, however, was not being splattered with red splotches in front of the whole class. And I did not like Mr. Green.

* * *

"Let me get this straight," Davis said. "You want me to do a story on the menu in the school cafeteria?" He stared at Ross in disbelief.

It was lunchtime and we were having an editorial meeting in the school newspaper office. "How does the cafeteria menu even qualify as news?" Davis wanted to know. He was wearing sunglasses. They were pushed partway down his nose and he was peering over the tops of them.

It was a good question, even though, personally, I liked the idea of Ross assigning the story to Davis, mainly because if he had to do the story, I didn't. I could tell by glancing around the room that the rest of the *Herald* staff felt the same way.

19

It was such a stupid idea — another of the endless school-focused, so-called news stories that Ms. Peters insisted we include in the *Herald* line-up.

"The Eat Smart menu was introduced after Christmas as a result of lobbying by students," Ross explained. He had to explain because Davis had transferred to East Hastings Regional less than two months ago, which meant that Eat Smart pre-dated him. "Now would be a good time to see whether it's been a success."

I doubt that I was alone in noticing Ross's lack of enthusiasm. He could be such a brown-noser with Ms. Peters sometimes, but even he knew the difference between news and fluff.

The idea behind Eat Smart had been to get rid of "bad" foods, like hamburgers, pizza slices, french fries and gravy, and prepackaged snack cakes, and to introduce "good" foods like veggie burgers, wrap sandwiches with hummus and bean sprouts, carrot and celery sticks, and fresh fruit. Although I hadn't actively lobbied for the change, I had signed the petition and I was glad that it had gone through.

"You might want to check out Ralph's," I said to Davis. Ralph's was a hole-in-the-wall greasy spoon a couple of blocks from school. On the menu at Ralph's were hamburgers, pizza slices, and fries with gravy. Ralph also had a fine selection of prepackaged snack cakes. "You might find the whole football team down there."

"You *will* find the whole football team down

there," Eric Moore said. Eric was our sports editor.

"Even assuming I'd set foot in that rat trap," Davis said, "I'm not *checking out* Ralph's because I'm *not* doing the story. It's the most rinky-dink, hick-town idea I've heard since I got here."

Davis liked to remind us that he did not come from a hick town. He came from Toronto. I think that was supposed to explain how he got to be so cool. Davis had discovered that life in a small town was different from life in the big, sophisticated city. He resented this difference and held everyone in East Hastings responsible.

"Look, Davis, the way things work here — " Ross began.

"I'm sick of hearing about the way things work here. Back at my old school in Toronto — "

"Speaking of being sick," I muttered.

Davis turned on me. "You think you're so smart!" he said. "A cop's daughter! I've heard what they're calling you — little Miss Perfect, who cheats on tests!"

"Excuse me?" I said, a little stunned by this outburst. And what did he mean, *they?* I thought it was just Rick.

"Ever since I got here, you've been trashing me — where I come from, my old school, my reputation."

I let the first two slide. I mean, Toronto and a Richie Rich private school — who wouldn't trash that combination?

"What reputation?" I said. "As far as I can tell,

you're a legend in your own mind and nowhere else."

His eyes burned into mine. "I guess that explains all the awards I've won," he said. "I went to a real school, not an armpit like this yokel central. And we had a real newspaper that covered real issues which, for your information, did not include cafeteria menus."

Apparently Davis's old school had potloads of money. Apparently the father of one of the kids was some big deal newspaper publisher. Apparently that accounted for the existence of a *real* and well-financed newspaper. Too bad for Davis, though — his parents had gone through a nasty divorce. His mother had fought for and gotten custody of Davis. She had uprooted him from his exclusive neighborhood and "dragged" him up to East Hastings, as Davis liked to put it, so that she could recover from her divorce while looking after her elderly and ailing mother. Poor, poor Davis.

"The way things work here," Ross said, wading wearily into the fray — he had grown mighty weary of Davis — "is that you take the story you're assigned."

"Can't a person pitch a story idea around here? That's how I got to write that series on street kids down on — "

"Yonge Street," I said. "We heard."

He had actually lived as a street kid for a few days, panhandling with them, hanging with them, crashing with them. Even I had to admit that it was a good idea. I would have said so to Davis, too, if he hadn't been always boasting about it. So instead, I said, *"Anybody* can make a story out of stuff that's sensational, Davis. But to make a story out of a cafeteria menu, now *that* would be a real accomplishment."

Davis glowered at me. "I only write about things that matter, things I care about, things I can really immerse myself in. I'm an investigative reporter, not a hack journalist. I won an award for my series of articles on the alternative music scene in Toronto," he added, as if everyone in the room didn't already know.

"In that case," Ross said, "maybe we should put your award-winning knowledge of music to good use and have you cover the choir competition. The school choir came in first at the regionals and is getting ready for the provincials — "

"I'd rather have all my teeth pulled," Davis said. "Without Novocain. How about if I do a story on the so-called punk scene up in Dweebsville." Davis thought Morris was a dweeby name, so he found it amusing to refer to Morrisville as Dweebsville.

"Ixnay," Ross said.

"Ixnay? What's that, ixnay?"

"It means no," Mark Goulbert informed him. Mark drew cartoons for the paper. He was pretty good at it.

"Why not?"

"Because we cover the news at East Hastings Regional, not the news in Morrisville," I said. I meant it as kind of a jab at Ross. I had suggested my share of stories only to have them turned down on the basis that we covered all the news that was fit to print at our school, forget that we lived in a town, let alone a whole country, and don't even get me started on the planet. Half the time the biggest challenge a *Herald* reporter had was trying to stay awake on assignment. But I guess Davis missed my sarcasm because he looked at me as if I were some bottom-rung corporate flack spouting the company line.

"Okay," he said. "How about a story on cheating? Better yet, how about a story on the local cop's kid cheating on a test? Oh, no, wait a minute, that's probably not news!"

"Hey!" I said. All of a sudden, every time someone wanted to take a jab at me, they brought up the cheating thing.

"Hey, Davis, relax. This kind of fighting isn't useful," Ross said. He was struggling to stay calm.

"This so-called newspaper isn't useful," Davis said. "It's the most boring rag I ever fell asleep over." I wasn't unsympathetic to his point, just to his personality. "Hey, I have another idea," he said. "Why don't you do a readership survey? Why don't you actually *ask* people what they think of the *Herald*?"

Ross started to look a little defensive.

"I don't have a problem with that," Eric said. There was no reason why he should. Everyone liked sports. Almost everyone — certainly one hundred percent of the people who cared about football

— was proud of East Hastings Regional's football team, which routinely won regional championships. Eric could get downright poetic when he wrote about them, which meant that the sports pages were well read.

"We're *not* doing a readership survey," Ross said. "We have better things to do with our time."

"Yeah, like asking people if they like veggie burgers," Davis said.

"Students at this school demanded change," Ross said. "They got it and we have a duty to report on it. Your deadline is next Friday."

"No, it isn't," Davis said. "I don't have to put up with this. I'm working on a movie script. I've got a real shot at the summer program at the Canadian Film Institute. This guy I know — "

"Not the movie script again," someone said. It wasn't me. It was Eric. We'd all heard as much about the movie script as we had about Davis's award-winning student newspaper articles and the movie he'd made — a video, really — that had won some student contest. Apparently the father of one of his old school buddies was a movie producer and had seen it. Apparently he was encouraging Davis. Apparently there was no end to Davis's brilliance.

"I'm out of here," Davis said. "I quit."

Funny thing, no one tried to talk him out of it. If he stopped working on the paper, he'd have to work on the school literary journal or the yearbook. Poor, poor literary journal. Poor, poor yearbook.

"I hate to say it," I said, after Davis stormed out of the newspaper office, "but he has a point. This would be a much more interesting newspaper if we could cover things people actually care about."

"Well, we can't," Ross said. We all stared at him. "What I mean is, students care about what goes on in this school," he said. "If they want to read about other stuff, they can read other papers."

"Why can't we change that? Why can't we write about all of the things that interest people at this school? Why do we have to stick to what actually happens *in* the school?"

"That's just the way it is," Ross said.

"Chloe has a point," Mark Goulbert said. "A school newspaper doesn't necessarily have to be *about* school."

"But Ms. Peters — " Ross began. He was beginning more sentences than he was finishing today.

"Maybe Davis's idea for a readership survey isn't so bad," I said. "Maybe if we ask people and they say they want a change, we can convince Ms. Peters." Actually, it sounded like a good idea. "We could run a short survey in the next issue. We could design it so that people can clip it out and drop it in a box."

"Like a ballot box," Mark said.

"I could design the survey with dotted lines and a little pair of scissors, so people get the idea," Aiysha Winston said. Aiysha did layout and design for the paper.

"I have no problem with that," Eric said. He had

a faraway look in his eyes, as if he were imagining the *Herald* morphing into *Sports Illustrated North*. Eric was a jock who drew top marks in English. He wanted to be a real sportswriter in the worst way. He had a job covering the local sports scene for the East Hastings and Region *Beacon*, which came out twice a week. It didn't pay much, but it did pay.

The feeling was unanimous — well, almost unanimous — and in the end we agreed to try it.

"This isn't an attack on *you*," I told Ross, after the meeting had ended. "People think you're doing a good job."

"Which is why they want to change everything," he grumbled.

"Change is a good thing, Ross. It's nothing personal."

"Yeah, sure. Oh, by the way, I'm assigning you the cafeteria story. Nothing personal."

* * *

Mr. Green dropped in to check that I was serving my detention. I had my history text open in front of me and was doing my reading for his class. That should have made him happy. It always made Mr. Lawry happy to see students reading history books. But it only seemed to annoy Mr. Green.

"This is supposed to be a detention," he said to Mr. Azoulay, who was on detention hall duty this week.

Mr. Azoulay looked startled as he glanced up from the stack of papers he was marking. I think he was expecting to find that all of his detainees had fled. But no, we were still there, Dean Abbott, Morgan Hicks (for whom detention was a regular gig), Brad Hudson, and little old me.

"It *is* a detention," Mr. Azoulay said.

"But they're doing homework." Mr. Green nodded pointedly at me.

Mr. Azoulay looked puzzled and didn't say anything. I didn't understand the problem either.

"Detention is supposed to be a punishment," Mr. Green said. "How can it be a punishment if it means they can get all their homework done and end up with a free evening? When I was in school, you got extra work to do in detention, like copying a page out of the dictionary. Then you still had your homework to complete when you got home."

For a young guy, Mr. Green was an old fogey. The next thing we knew, he'd be telling us about trudging five miles — no, make that *ten* miles — to school, in snow up to his waist.

Mr. Azoulay looked at Dean Abbott, Morgan Hicks, Brad Hudson and me, all with textbooks open in front of us, all with pens in hand, all actually — or at least apparently — working. The fact that we were using our time to do homework didn't seem to trouble him. Just the opposite. He looked at Mr. Green. "Thanks for your input," he said.

We all cracked up. Mr. Green's face turned splotchy red and he retreated from the room. He was back five minutes later with Ms. Jeffries. I found myself in the office again, sitting on the bench, waiting for Levesque. I was in trouble. Only it wasn't for anything that had happened in detention. It was for something that had happened in the school parking lot.

Chapter 3

Levesque was sitting on my right, Mr. Green on my left, and Ms. Jeffries was at her desk directly opposite me. They were all looking at me.

"I didn't do it," I said.

I had to fight to keep my temper under control. I had been accused of puncturing one of the tires on Mr. Green's car. It was Mr. Green who had accused me.

"So it's just a coincidence that I found this jammed into the hole in my tire?" Mr. Green said. He held up a purple ballpoint pen, the same kind that I always used.

"You think someone punctured your tire with a plastic ballpoint pen?" I said. Like that was even remotely possible. Trying to puncture a tire with a ballpoint would be like trying to puncture steel with a bobby pin.

"I think *someone* was making a statement," Mr. Green said.

"How stupid do you think I am?" I said. My anger was getting the better of me. "Do you really think if I was going to puncture your tire, I'd stick something into the hole that would make you suspect me?"

"That's a pretty good question," Levesque observed. He had settled into his chair and was acting far too calm to suit me. I would have appreciated a little righteous indignation.

"Look, Mr. Levesque," Mr. Green began.

"*Chief* Levesque," Levesque said, which surprised me. He usually didn't pull rank on people unless he was acting in his official capacity. "I understand you live in Elder Bay, Mr. Green." This was news to me. Levesque had obviously done his homework. "So I wouldn't expect you to know this, but I'm chief of police here in East Hastings." He said this in a conversational way, the way he might say, "How about those Leafs?" but he was watching Mr. Green more intently than someone who was interested only in small talk.

A red splotch appeared on Mr. Green's neck. Good.

"This wouldn't be the first time a police officer's child got into trouble," Mr. Green said. "Have you ever considered that your daughter's actions in my class might be her way of rebelling against you as an authority figure?"

Levesque seemed to mull over this question for a moment. Then he said, "No, I can't say that I have."

"Well, maybe you should," Mr. Green said. "I majored in psychology, Mr. — Chief Levesque.

Child psychology. It was that interest that led me to teaching."

"I see," Levesque said. "And did you see Chloe puncture your tire?"

"No, I didn't, but her behavior in my class would suggest — "

"Did *anyone* see her puncture your tire?"

More splotches had massed on Mr. Green's neck and were now staging an assault on his face.

"Not that I'm aware of, but — "

"Have you asked if anyone saw Chloe, or anyone else for that matter, vandalizing your car?"

"No, I haven't," Mr. Green said. He was starting to sound angry.

"Louis, I asked you here because Mr. Green expressed some concerns about his relationship with Chloe," Ms. Jeffries said.

"Oh, I see," Levesque said. He sounded dead calm. "I thought you asked me here because Mr. Green is accusing Chloe of puncturing one of his tires."

"That's exactly right," Mr. Green said.

Ms. Jeffries shook her head.

"Nobody is accusing anyone of anything," she said. "We're just exploring a problem between a student and a teacher."

"She challenged my authority in class today."

I had done nothing of the kind. It was becoming obvious that Mr. Green just flat out didn't like me.

"You practically accused me of plagiarism!" I said.

Out of the corner of my eye, I saw Levesque shift in his chair.

"Let's deal with one thing at a time," he suggested. "Now then, is your car parked in the parking lot to the east of the school, or do you use some special parking place off school property?" He had switched to his this-means-business quiet voice, the one that makes you pay close attention because you don't want to miss a word.

"It's in the school parking lot."

"If I'm not mistaken, that lot holds about a hundred and fifty cars and it's usually full." Levesque glanced at Ms. Jeffries, who nodded. "Also, if I'm not mistaken, students routinely cut through the parking lot on their way to and from school, and to and from school buses." Again, Ms. Jeffries nodded. "In fact, it wouldn't be unusual for almost every student and every teacher in this building to set foot in that parking lot once a day. That's about fourteen hundred people, Mr. Green. That's a lot of people with access to your car."

"No one at this school has given me as much trouble as your daughter has."

"There are a few things you should know about Chloe," Levesque said. "First, she doesn't cheat. Second, you're right, she does have a tendency to defy authority. But it's been my general experience that she only does so when that authority is wielded inappropriately. Third, she speaks her mind, like it or not. If she has a problem with you, she'll tell you directly. She won't sneak around behind your back. Finally, whatever else she is, my daughter is not stupid."

That made me sit up straight. Technically, I wasn't his daughter. He was my stepfather, but he hadn't adopted me or anything. I tried to remember him ever referring to me as his daughter before, and drew a blank.

"If she were ever to do anything as stupid as vandalize a car," he continued, "you could be pretty sure she wouldn't leave a calling card. Now, if you'd like to notify the East Hastings Police Department officially, I'll send an officer over to take a look at your car. I'll have someone ask around, too, if that's what you want. But I'm not sure what else we can do, especially since what appears to be the key piece of evidence has been so badly handled." He nodded at the purple pen in Mr. Green's hand. Then he stood up.

"I don't know what we've accomplished here, Alice," he said to Ms. Jeffries, "but thank you for alerting me to the problem."

"Thank you for coming, Louis," she said. She looked as deflated as a hostess whose elegant cocktail party had turned into a street brawl.

Levesque and I walked together to the parking lot. There were only a couple of cars left in it. One had a deflated rear driver's-side tire. Levesque walked over to it. He squatted down and inspected it, but didn't touch anything. Then he stood up and turned back to the school. He didn't seem at all surprised to find Mr. Green staring out at him from a window.

"Come on," Levesque said. "I'll drive you home."

I nodded and started to chuck my backpack into the back seat of the squad car.

"Whoa!" Levesque said. "Be careful. I've got an impression on the back seat."

"A what?" I peeked into the back seat and saw a big cardboard box. There was something white inside it.

"A footwear impression," Levesque said. "From the break-in up near the lake."

I knelt on the front seat and leaned over to take a closer look. Sure enough, there was a white plaster impression in the box.

"What are you going to do with that?" I asked. "Are you and Steve going to check every pair of boots and shoes in town?"

"Sneakers."

I took another look.

"Okay, sneakers."

"Nikes."

I took another look, but I didn't see anything that specifically said Nike. "How do you know that?"

"Experience."

"Do you have any idea how many Nikes there are in my school alone?" I said.

"I could come up with a pretty fair estimate." He turned the car key in the ignition. "You know, that teacher of yours isn't necessarily a bad guy."

"Oh, right, thanks," I said. "Stick up for him, why don't you?"

"All I'm saying is, he could use a little more experience."

"A sense of fairness wouldn't kill him, either," I said.

Levesque laughed. "That often comes with experience."

"It's like some gigantic club, isn't it?" I said.

"What is?"

"Adulthood. Sure, you took my side back there in the office. But now that we're out here, you're going to bat for your team. You guys never want kids to see dissension in the ranks. It's like you're afraid if we don't respect one of you, we won't respect any of you."

He put his arm along the back of his seat so that he could turn to see where he was backing the car.

"Relax, Chloe," he said. "I'm just saying some people could use a little experience dealing with situations like this. That's all."

Some people?

As we were pulling out of the school parking lot, we passed Daria Dattillo and Rick Antonio. My social radar had obviously been malfunctioning because there seemed to be something going on between Daria and Rick that I hadn't noticed before. That was the only way to account for the fact that Rick's arm was slung casually over Daria's shoulder. Daria turned and looked directly at me as we passed. I'm pretty sure she smiled. I'm just as sure that it wasn't a friendly smile.

Chapter 4

News travels fast in a closed environment. When I got to school the next morning, everyone knew what had happened to Mr. Green's car. A lot of people congratulated me for it. I asked everyone if they had seen it happen. No one had — at least, no one admitted anything.

"Wish I'd thought of it myself," Dean Abbott said. "The guy's a major jerk."

"When good kids go bad, they really go bad," Rick said. He was one of those people who have a lame sense of humor, but a firm belief that they belong in the Comedy Hall of Fame. He laughed. The only other person who laughed was his locker room buddy, Brad.

Sarah Moran gave me a look that meant either that she was chewing on a mud pie or that she disapproved of what I had supposedly done.

At first I proclaimed my innocence, but after a while I gave up. Nobody believed me, anyway. I just smiled and kept my mouth shut. Unfortunately, I happened to be smiling following another big "congrats," this one from Morgan Hicks, when Mr. Green walked by. It didn't look good, but I didn't care. I hadn't done anything wrong. I was beginning to think those words should be tattooed across my forehead.

Between my first and second classes of the day, I saw Steve Denby heading for the school office. It must have been a slow crime day. Or maybe Levesque thought he had to send Steve to investigate. It wouldn't look good if the chief of police appeared to be covering up some malfeasance on the part of his stepdaughter. When I dropped my books at my locker at lunchtime before heading off to Ralph's, I saw Steve again, circulating through the halls, approaching groups of kids and talking to them. He looked relaxed. I wondered how long it had been since he had graduated. I also wondered if he would find out anything about the vandalism of Mr. Green's car. If he did, would he tell me? Then I saw Davis stride over to him, notebook and pen in hand. I watched from a distance as Davis removed his sunglasses and started talking. He seemed to be interviewing Steve, not the other way around. What was that all about?

As I left school property, I thought about what had been happening. Anyone could have punctured Mr. Green's tire — for any number of reasons. No one liked him. But the purple pen, combined with the crib sheet Mr. Green had found under my desk, also written in purple ink, made it look like I had something to do with it. But why?

Why was someone trying to get me in trouble with Mr. Green? More importantly, who? Dismally, there seemed to be a number of possibilities — Daria, Rick, Sarah, Davis . . . and those were just the people I'd rubbed the wrong way *recently*. Just what every girl wants, a list of potential enemies so long that she doesn't know where to start.

I trudged up the street and around the corner to a restaurant wedged between a sporting goods store and a body shop. Maybe restaurant isn't the best word to describe Ralph's. When I think of restaurants, I generally think of food more than, say, pinball machines, video games and pool tables. Not that Ralph didn't serve food. His menu included burgers (Ralphburgers, cheeseburgers, Canuck burgers topped with bacon and cheese, and, of course, the deluxe double Ralphburger), hot dogs (Ralphdogs, chili dogs and Canuck dogs topped with bacon and cheese), pizza slices, fries (gravy extra), milkshakes, pop and a vast assortment of packaged snacks — chips, pork rinds (who eats those things, anyway?), cheese twists, cakes, tarts, cupcakes and chocolate bars. But, taking up more space than the, *ahem*, dining area, was the entertainment area. This consisted of a big screen TV tuned to an all-sports network, two pool tables in the back, and, down one wall, three pinball machines and half a dozen video game terminals.

Ralph's clientele, at least at this time of day, seemed to consist of the entire East Hastings Regional football team and its assorted female hangers-on. I'd heard that the evening brought a whole different crowd to Ralph's — guys who spent more time with their cars than with their girl-friends, guys who liked to hunt, guys who liked to drink beer and play pool while keeping their eye on whatever hockey game or baseball game or football game was on the tube. I'd also heard that the local criminal element hung out at Ralph's. This consisted of people — guys — who ran up a couple of hundred dollars in parking tickets, forcing Levesque to "pay them a visit." It was also people — guys — who got into fistfights over sports bets. And people — maybe guys and maybe not — who did a little illegal buying and selling. Wherever you go, there's always some of that going on.

Brad Hudson was the first one to notice me. He nodded to Rick, who was sitting across the table from him, scarfing down fries and gravy, using his fingers to eat. Nestled beside him was Daria. She turned and looked right at me, head held high, as if she was saying, *I've got nothing to be ashamed of.* Whatever. Like I cared.

This assignment was not going to be fun. But I was here and I was not going to retreat just because I didn't have a friend in the place. Instead, I sighed, put another chalk mark in the "Reasons to Hate Davis Kaye" column on my personal score-board, and dug a notepad and pen from my bag.

Three of Ralph's booths were filled with guys from school. I could have picked one that didn't contain Rick, Brad and Daria. But what would have been the point? This was an eat-your-broccoli moment — I wasn't going to be allowed to leave the table until I'd choked down the green stuff on my plate. I wasn't going to get out of Ralph's until Rick had given me a hard time. How could he resist? Here he was, surrounded by his adoring fans, and here I was, saddled with this stupid assignment. Make that, incredibly stupid assignment. Davis was right. This wasn't journalism.

I marched past the first two booths and stopped at the one where Rick was sitting.

"Hey, Rick," Brad said, "is it my imagination or did the temperature just drop in here?"

Rick looked at me. Actually, he looked at the front of my sweater, which made me remember his attempt to "have fun" after the concert.

"Yeah, well, I got something to keep me warm now," he said. He put an arm around Daria and pulled her close. She kept her eyes on the table. Watching them, I wondered if they were the ones who had framed me.

"So, guys," I said, "I'm here to cover a hot story for the *Herald* — the new school cafeteria menu." I had decided on a "Yeah, I know this is totally pathetic" approach. If I admitted it right up front, it might take the edge off the jazzing they were sure to give me. "Correct me if I'm wrong, but up until Christmas, you guys used to hold down the back corner of the cafeteria at lunchtime," I said. "You seem to have deserted it about the same time the Eat Smart menu came in."

"Eat fart menu, you mean," Brad said. The whole table, except Daria, laughed at this reference to the three-bean salads and the bean burritos that had appeared on the cafeteria menu. I made a note of his comment.

I turned to Rick. From the superior look on his face, you would have thought I was down on my knees begging him to ask me out again.

"What do you think of the new Eat Smart menu?" I asked him.

Rick shook his head. "And here I thought you were such a genius," he said. "Doesn't this tell you anything?" He waved a hand around the place. Then he said, "No, wait a minute, you're not a genius after all, are you? I mean, you cheated on that history test."

With a little help from my friends, I thought. I gestured at the remains of fries and gravy on his plate.

"Don't you worry about what you put in your body?" I asked. Not that I cared. If he wanted to pack his body full of dynamite and light the fuse, that would have been fine with me.

"I need my carbs," he said. "I'm an athlete." He pronounced it *ath-a-lete*.

"If the school ditched the new menu, would you go back?" I asked.

He shrugged. "If the school ditched the new menu and put in a pool table, I might consider it."

This was greeted by what sounded like grunts of approval from the rest of the football team. I made a note of that — sound effects might add some color to an otherwise stupid article. Then I looked at Daria's plate, which held a barely touched slice of pepperoni pizza glistening with grease.

"What about you?" I asked. "Do you like the food here?"

"She's not here for the food," Rick said, and slung his arm around her again.

I ignored him.

"It's okay, I guess," she said. She didn't look at me. She hated to look at me. I wanted to shake her. I hadn't done anything to her — well, nothing that she hadn't done to herself first.

I shuffled down to the next booth to get a few more quotes. I heard the door open and close behind me, and someone blew by me and headed for the back where the pool tables were. It was Davis. He stood in the deserted back room for a minute, looking around, then turned and hurried back to the door. He glanced at me, but didn't say anything. I guess he'd changed his mind about setting foot in this rat-trap.

* * *

I stopped by the newspaper office before classes started again.

"How come you assigned Davis to cover the punctured tire story?" I asked Ross. It didn't seem fair. Davis had turned down the cafeteria story, which I was now stuck with, and had ended up with a better assignment.

"I didn't," Ross said. "He quit the paper, remember?"

"But I saw him covering it. He was talking to Steve Denby."

"Not for this paper," Ross said.

Eric Moore looked up from his computer. "He's probably covering it for the *Beacon*," he said.

"Davis works for the *Beacon*?"

Eric nodded. "I was delivering my column when he came in to talk to Mr. Torelli." Mr. Torelli was the *Beacon*'s owner, publisher, editor, reporter and advertising sales manager. I think he was even its chief delivery person. "He made a pretty good pitch."

"He did?"

"He said most parents have no clue what's going on in the one place where their kids spend most of their time. He said *Beacon* readers would probably appreciate a regular column on the school, school events and school issues. He showed Mr. Torelli some articles he wrote for his school paper back in Toronto and, boom, Mr. Torelli hired him on the spot."

I heard a slapping sound. It was Ross's hand smacking Ross's forehead. "Why didn't I think of that?" he said.

Even I had to admit it was a good idea. Of course, I didn't say that to Davis when I ran into him on my way home. Actually, I didn't do the running. He did. I was leaving school property when I heard someone call my name. I turned and saw Davis hurrying to catch up to me. Standing behind him, watching him, was Sarah Moran. Our eyes met.

Then hers shifted back to Davis. I didn't need Cupid to tell me that Sarah's interest in Davis was more than casual. Geez, had the whole world fallen in love when I wasn't looking?

"I need to talk to you," Davis said, clutching a reporter's notebook in one hand.

"About what?"

"Is it true you punctured Mr. Green's tire?"

I liked that — the direct approach to investigative reporting.

"Do you think I'd tell you if I had?" I said.

He wrote that down.

"I'm not talking on the record, Davis," I said.

"If you're talking, it's on the record."

"Fine. Then I'm not talking."

"Some people saw you in the parking lot that day," he said.

"Big deal. I'm in the parking lot almost every day. So is most of the school. Why don't you ask me who I saw in the parking lot?"

"What about the purple pen?"

"What about it?"

"You write with a purple pen. Same brand, from what I've heard."

"Same brand as you can buy in half a dozen places around here."

"Mr. Green doesn't like you."

I had to bite my tongue to keep myself from pointing out that the feeling was mutual.

"I talked to a lot of people today who said you didn't deny that you'd done it."

"I'm not really interested in talking about it, Davis."

"Refusing to answer?"

"Refusing to answer," I confirmed. Then, mostly because he was so annoying, I said, "You really hit the big time, huh, Davis? Quit the *Herald* so you could tackle major investigative pieces for the *Beacon*. Looks like all that big city experience of yours is coming in really handy now."

He kept smiling at me, but his eyes grew unfriendly.

"You don't know anything about anything," he said. "Maybe I'm working on something really big. Maybe I'm lining myself up for something that'll win awards."

Just what the world needed — more awards for Davis.

"Yeah, well, keep me posted," I said.

He flipped his notebook shut. "For what it's worth," he said, "I think Mr. Green is a jerk, too. You get points in my book for every bit of grief you give him. A lot of people told me the same thing."

"Gosh, thanks, Davis," I said. Sarcastically. "You have no idea what that means to me."

* * *

I headed home alone, taking the long route through the south end of East Hastings Provincial Park. It had been a tough week and I was in a bad mood, even if it was technically the weekend. When I'm in a rotten mood, walking helps. Especially when I'm walking where I'm not likely to run into anyone else, where my mind can wander, where I can hear birdsong instead of car horns, and smell cedar and pine instead of car exhaust.

I crossed Lodge Lake Road, leaving the last of East Hastings's houses behind, and headed up to 42 Sideroad, which ran through the southern tip of the park. It was peaceful on the dirt and gravel road. That wasn't surprising, given that it was only April. Hardly any cottage owners came up during the off-season. Most wouldn't open their places until the Victoria Day weekend at the end of May, which meant that right now traffic was practically nil.

I slowed as I approached the park entrance. To the west of it there was a paved rest area where cars could pull over. In summertime, park authorities put out picnic tables and garbage cans. A phone booth stood at the end of the rest area farthest from me. A car was parked on the side of the road near it. A man stood in the booth, holding the receiver with one hand while his other hand sliced and diced the air in front of him. I heard the bark of his voice, but couldn't make out his words. I was glad that I wasn't on the other end of the line, though. Whoever he was talking to was getting a real earful.

The man turned his head as I got closer. He glowered at me, as if I were invading his solitude. But he got no sympathy from me. If you want to be alone, don't stand in a public place, I thought. Still, I picked up my pace. I don't like to hang around where I'm not wanted. I had the feeling that the guy was following me with his eyes, but it was probably just that — a feeling. I slowed a little when I drew even with his car. Nice, I thought. It was a cream-colored Jaguar with, whoa, butter-cream upholstery that looked like real leather. It was well cared for too. There wasn't a single smudge or spot on it. Hmmm, nestled in a holder right next to the car radio was a cell phone. I wondered why Mr. Privacy Hound didn't just use the phone in his car. I turned to look back at him. Big mistake.

It hadn't been just a feeling. He *had* been watching me. As I turned, he slammed down the receiver and ripped open the door to the phone booth. He came out of that booth like a hunger-crazed bear charging out of a cave after hibernation. Geez, what did he think I was going to do? Steal his car while he stood there watching?

"Hey!" he roared at me. "Hey, you, get away from there!"

I admit I was a little scared. I was in the middle of pretty much nowhere and a ticked-off stranger was rushing toward me. I thrust both hands into the air — look at me, I'm harmless, really, I'm *defenseless*. Then something clicked in my brain. I was in the middle of pretty much nowhere and a ticked-off stranger was rushing toward me. Maybe sending off defenseless signals wasn't the smartest thing to do.

I jumped the ditch at the roadside and headed

into the park, off-trail. Headed? Ran. *Raced.* I knew where I was going — sort of. If I kept in a straight line, I'd hit one of the park trails. Sure enough, I did. Only then did I glance back over my shoulder. No one had followed me. I stayed on the trail until I reached the eastern edge of the park, then I cut back onto 42 Sideroad, cautiously. There was no sign of the man or his Jaguar. Still, I walked home a little faster than usual and was gladder than usual to get there. What a week!

Levesque got home just as I was loading the supper dishes into the dishwasher. Phoebe and I had made one of our favorite meals — cream of mushroom soup and grilled cheese sandwiches. I offered to make a sandwich for him. He accepted. While I cooked, I asked him if Steve had found out anything about Mr. Green's car. He shook his head.

"It's a big school with a lot of traffic," he said. "So far as I know, he hasn't turned up anything useful yet."

"Yet? How much time is he going to spend on this?"

Levesque rolled his wide shoulders in a shrug. "Mr. Green made a complaint. We have to look into it, especially under the circumstances."

Those circumstances, I knew, were me.

"You know I didn't do it," I said.

He swallowed a bite of sandwich and reached for his glass of milk. "Someone did," he said.

Chapter 5

Some weekends — rainy weekends, cold weekends, gray November weekends — are made for hunkering down, burrowing into a pile of books, and researching and writing an essay. This wasn't one of those weekends. It was agony to confine myself to the public library on Saturday afternoon. It wasn't made any easier by the fact that I seemed to be the only person in town doing schoolwork and the only person in my history class slogging away on my essay.

As I sat by the big front window, making notes from half a dozen books, I saw Ross stroll by with his little sister. She was in her Brownie uniform, so I guess he was taking her to or from some Brownie event. I saw Dean Abbott and Morgan Hicks going by in fairly good repair around noon and swinging by again, tattered and dirt-stained, a few hours later. A pickup football game would have been my guess. Davis buzzed back and forth a couple of times. Once I saw him go into the *Beacon* office. Another time he came out carrying a bag from

Stella's Great Home Cooking and talking with some guy I didn't recognize. They were chatting about something and kept talking while the guy unchained a big black dog that had been lying on the sidewalk. The dog was wearing a muzzle, which told *me* something, but obviously didn't say much to Davis. He reached down to pat it. The dog lunged at him. Like an Olympic long jumper in reverse, Davis leapt backward, his patting hand high over his head. I guessed there hadn't been many canines in Davis's life. Anyone who knows anything about dogs knows you don't touch an animal you're not acquainted with, especially a mean-looking one. Especially when its owner feels the need to keep it muzzled. Later, as I was gathering up my stuff to go home, Davis strolled by again, this time with Sarah Moran. Her head was turned toward him. He seemed to be doing all the talking. She seemed to be listening raptly. Maybe he was telling her all about his screenplay.

Even Daria was enjoying the warm spring weather. I saw her go into the drugstore, then Stedman's and the Book Nook. Every time she reappeared on the sidewalk, she was carrying another bag. Later I saw her walking hand in hand with Rick. Obviously she wasn't a great judge of character. She liked Rick, but she didn't like me. Oh well, nobody's perfect.

While all of East Hastings played, I worked. I was probably more motivated than anyone else when it came to this particular essay, though. I didn't want to just do well. I wanted to write the best fifteen-hundred-word essay that Mr. Green had ever read. And since this was his first year teaching and he probably hadn't read many fifteen-hundred-word essays yet, I also wanted it to be the best one he would ever read. But that didn't stop me from peering wistfully out the window every now and again.

Sunday didn't even try to make my job easier. The sun had pierced my bedroom curtains by the time I was jangled awake by a ringing telephone. I squinted at my clock — it wasn't even nine yet — and closed my eyes again, but they wouldn't stay closed. The twin fragrances of coffee and toast were beckoning me. I pulled on a robe and stumbled down the stairs. The coffee pot was almost full. Two pieces of toast stood at attention in the old-fashioned toaster we'd had since before I was born. Levesque was lacing up his shoes.

"Leaving?" I asked.

He nodded.

"Work?"

"Another cottage break-in," he said, straightening up. "I don't know when I'll be back."

"No problem," I said.

After he left, I poured myself a cup of coffee and made some fresh toast. I thought about all the things I could do on an April Sunday. Then I settled down to my essay — for a couple of hours. Finally, though, enough was enough.

"Where are you going?" Phoebe asked.

"Out."

"Where?"

Little sisters can be annoying, especially when they start acting like mothers.

"Out," I said again. "See you later."

I can stand being cooped up inside for only so long. I headed due west, across the railway tracks and straight into the park. I hadn't been much of a nature lover back home in Montreal. But since we'd moved up here, I had discovered that I liked hiking and exploring the woods. I had also discovered a few favorite places. The best was a section of the provincial park that the park authorities had reportedly been having anxiety attacks over for the past couple of years, ever since a nasty accident.

The general area was called Puzzle Rock. It consisted of a gigantic limestone formation that rose out of nowhere to a height of fifteen or twenty feet. The mammoth rock was so fissured that from above it looked like someone had taken a slab of rock and dropped it, shattering it into a couple of hundred pieces, the way a dropped plate shatters on a tiled floor. The fissures were as deep as the height of the rock and ran off in all directions. In some places the space between rock faces was only five or six inches. In other places it was much greater. Some fissures started off wide enough to accommodate a person, but then got narrower and narrower until they suddenly dead-ended. Others spidered clear through the huge limestone formation. The nasty accident that kept park authorities up nights was a little boy who had fallen into one of the fissures, hit rock bottom, and ended up in a coma. He eventually recovered, but afterwards all the park's hiking trails were altered so that they no longer led to Puzzle Rock. Mention of it was also removed from the park maps that were given out to tourists. I had only found it because Ross showed it to me. When he did, it was love at first sight.

The top of the formation was covered with tall, ancient cedar trees. How they managed to grow on sheer rock, I don't know. But they did. From the sides of the fissures, you could see their roots burrowing deep into the limestone. It was a kind of minor miracle.

The place drew me again and again. Once I had the bright idea to explore the fissures. I stepped into a narrow gap between two rock walls and followed along until it got tighter and tighter. Finally I had to turn back. I thought I was headed back the way I had come, but I wasn't. I ended up in another dead end, then another and another. Then I started to panic. What if I couldn't find my way out? What if it got dark and I was still stuck in there? What if no one found me? What if I died in there?

It took me maybe an hour to find my way out and by then I was drenched in sweat, even though it was clear and cold that day. I hurried home as fast as I could. But the next day I came back. This time I climbed to the top of the formation and explored it from above. That's when I made my big discovery. I don't know how nature could have planned it, so it must have been a coincidence — another minor miracle. What I discovered was that if you entered from the south and stayed to the right every time two fissures came together, you could follow a winding path right through to the other side of the formation without any problem. I tested it and when it worked, I felt like I had uncovered the mystery of the universe. I tested it again and again. I'd figured it out! Me, the city girl! I scraped a mark into the limestone at the entry point, but I didn't tell anyone about it. It was my secret.

I headed for Puzzle Rock that Sunday. When I got there, I climbed to the top and sat down to enjoy the view. I hadn't been there more than twenty tranquil minutes when I heard someone. I looked in the general direction of the most creative compilation of bad words I had heard in a long time. A few yards southeast of Puzzle Rock, I spotted Davis. He was turning around and around, like a slow-spinning top. He muttered again. I debated whether or not to make myself invisible, then, finally, I called down to him.

"Problem?"

He peered up at me, shading his eyes with one hand.

I stood up so he could see me better.

"Oh," he said. "It's you."

His enthusiasm was underwhelming.

"Fine," I said. I retreated from view.

"No, hey, wait!" he called, his voice thick with panic.

I stepped into sight again and waited.

"Okay, so I'm lost, so big deal," he said. He made it sound like it was my fault.

I waited some more.

"Can you at least point me in the right direction?" he said, with typical male reluctance. What is it with guys and directions?

"I could," I said. "But it sort of depends on where you want to go."

"Out of here," he said. "I want to get out of this armpit and back to civilization. I don't know how anyone with half a brain can live up here for more than five minutes and not die of boredom. You people have no idea what you're missing."

Right. Like living in East Hastings was like living in Siberia or something. And, given the Internet, satellite dishes and technology in general, even people in Siberia had a pretty good idea what was going on in the rest of the world. I was tempted to direct Davis into the maze of fissures and let him try to find his way out again, just so he'd know what he'd been missing.

"Walk due south until you hit the trail," I said. "Then follow it."

His face twisted into a dopey-looking question mark.

"South," I repeated. "That way." I pointed.

He nodded. Then he studied his surroundings a little more closely.

"What is this, anyway?" he said, approaching one of the fissures. "Does this go anywhere?"

"Yeah," I said. "In circles. If you go in, you'll get lost and never get out again."

His expression shifted. He was trying to decide whether or not to believe me.

"Be my guest," I said. "Go on in and see how long it takes you to get back out."

He backed away from the fissures and, instead, climbed up to where I was.

"Wow," he said, as he gazed around.

Wow, I thought. Now I've seen and heard everything. Mr. I'm-So-Cool-Big-City-Guy actually seemed impressed by something he had seen way up here in East Armpit.

"I see what you mean," he said, looking down.

"I gotta go," I said.

"Can you really get lost in there?"

"Yeah, you can," I said.

"Next I suppose you're going to tell me that all you locals know your way around blindfolded," he said.

"For your information, I'm not a local," I told him. "I moved here a few months ago from Montreal." Okay, so it was more like nine months, which, technically, is more than a few.

He seemed less than impressed.

"You got local real fast," he said.

"I take an interest."

"So, do you?"

"Do I what?"

"Know your way around this place?" He nodded to the closest fissure.

"So what if I do?"

He grinned as if he'd scored a point off me. "Yeah," he said, "you're local."

"I hope you can walk a straight line, Davis," I said. "A lot of people think they can, but once they're in the trees where everything looks the same, they find out they can't. If you don't stay headed due south, if you drift even a little, you're going to end up nowhere near the trail. And without the trail, it's going to take you a while to get out of the park."

I climbed back down the way I had come.

"Hey!" he called.

"Due south," I said, and pointed once more.

"I know what you're thinking," he said. "You're thinking, stupid city kid." Gee, and he was psychic, too. "You're wrong, you know."

"I don't care." Never had three truer words been spoken.

"Yeah, well, enjoy it while you can. I'm a quick study. You can only do this to me once."

"Bon voyage," I called, then disappeared into the trees as fast as I could. He probably wouldn't have much trouble finding the trail. It wasn't that far. But he might sweat a little in the five minutes it would take him to get there. And that might do him a little good. Then again, it might not. The truth was, it would take a lifetime and a half of saunas to make Davis Kaye sweat enough to make him

even remotely tolerable.

* * *

I smelled apple pie when I walked through the front door. Apple pie was Levesque's favorite dessert, which was why Phoebe had made it. Phoebe was always sucking up to him. She was determined to turn herself into the perfect daughter of a guy who wasn't really her father. But, hey, if it meant we had pie for dessert, I wasn't going to complain. In fact, I even pitched in to help her with the rest of supper. Levesque or no Levesque, we had to eat, and I was hungry.

"Why don't we make Mom's chicken, mushroom and rice casserole?" I said.

Phoebe grinned. She put on a couple of CDs and we worked together in the kitchen. We didn't argue even once. Levesque appeared right on cue just as the timer went off. I heard him taking off his shoes in the front hall. He came into the kitchen sniffing. Then he saw the pie and his eyes lit up.

"I could eat a horse," he said.

"You'll have to settle for chicken," I said.

Phoebe was buzzing around, setting the dining room table. She took a pair of Mom's silver candlesticks from the china cabinet, set them in the middle of the table, and lit candles.

"It's Sunday dinner," she said, when I gave her a look. "Sunday dinner is supposed to be special."

When we were little, we were just as likely to spend Sunday dinner with a baby-sitter as with our mother. Before Mom met Levesque, she had worked as a waitress. She'd put in long hours. After she met Levesque, when we were still living in Montreal, there was a better-than-even chance that he wouldn't be around for a meal any night of the week, never mind Sunday dinner. Up here, though, things were different. Sure, he still had to dash out at odd times every now and then. But for some reason the crime rate, never fantastically high, dropped out of sight about the time roasts were coming out of ovens on Sundays. Levesque was almost always around for Sunday dinner, which made Mom gooey-eyed and inspired Phoebe to master pie making.

"So, how was your day?" I asked, after I'd served the casserole and passed the salad.

He shrugged. "It would be better if people were more careful about securing their cottages before they headed south for the winter," he said. "A three-year-old could jimmy some of those locks." He sounded disgusted.

"It's not even cottage season yet," I said. Most cottages up here were set far back in the woods or on the edges of lakes. You couldn't see them from the road. "How did you find out about the break-ins?"

That earned me a big sigh. "We're going to have to do the circuit for exactly that reason," he said. "Three break-ins have been reported so far. But for all we know, there could be more that no one has noticed yet. The first one was discovered by a man out walking his dog. He saw an open screen door and went to investigate. The second one was reported by a group of hikers from Toronto. They spotted an open window."

"They were hiking in someone's yard?" Phoebe said.

"The hiking trail runs through private property in a few places," Levesque said. "With the owners' permission. The place looked closed up, but they saw that a window was open."

"Sounds pretty careless," I said, "breaking into a place, then leaving a window open so that it's obvious you've broken in."

Levesque didn't say anything. He seemed to be thinking.

"So, what about the third one?" I said finally. No answer. "You said there were *three* break-ins. What was that — open door or open window?" Still no answer, which could only mean one thing. "It was different, huh?"

For a few moments, nothing. Then, "We heard about the third one from a man who had been contracted by the owners to do some pre-season work," he said. It sounded more like he was talking to himself than answering my question. "He noticed that someone had been in the place recently, and he had heard about the other break-ins, so he called us."

"How could he tell?" I said.

"He saw a footprint in the kitchen."

I tried to picture this and frowned. "Maybe the owners didn't clean up before they left for the season."

Levesque shook his head. "It was a partial, muddy footprint on the kitchen floor. The fact that it was still wet meant that it couldn't have been there for long."

"Was anything taken?"

Again he shook his head. "We're not sure. Most people don't keep a lot of valuables in their cottages. Even the televisions are old. Two of the places had VCRs, but they weren't expensive and hadn't been touched. There was some evidence that drawers and closets had been gone through. I've talked to all of the owners. They all said the same thing — the most valuable things are their boats and motors, and in all three cases, they were locked up and hadn't been touched, either."

"If the thieves aren't taking anything valuable, why are they bothering to break in?" Phoebe asked.

"If they're not taking anything, you can't really call them thieves," I pointed out.

"You think they're looking for something?" Phoebe said.

"You've got me," Levesque said. "Is there any more casserole? It's really good."

I couldn't help it. I felt pleased.

Chapter 6

The Monday morning edition of the East Hastings *Beacon* was on our porch when I left for school in the morning. I picked it up and tossed it into the front hall. It wasn't a great paper, but I usually got a kick out of its weekly roundup of local criminal activity. It's not exactly the *National Enquirer*, but it's entertaining. Apart from a couple of recent murders, crime in East Hastings consisted mainly of small stuff — a little vandalism here, a little rowdyism there, here a drunk and disorderly, there a late-night dust-up.

Once there was a rash of shoplifting, another time someone smashed three Coke machines around town in an attempt to rob them. But it was fun to read about because Mr. Torelli played it up as if criminal masterminds were hard at work in town. He'd run a headline that said, *Gang Threatens Downtown Peace*, but when you read the article, it turned out that "gang" was used as a synonym for "group" and didn't mean the kind of gang you'd read about in, say, Los Angeles or New York.

"Downtown" meant the intersection of Dundas and Centre Streets, which is anchored by a bank and a Canadian Tire store. "Peace" meant the routine boredom of small-town life, which was "threatened" by a group of teenage boys who were trying to alleviate that boredom by acting tough with each other. The crime column ran on Mondays because most criminal activity in East Hastings happened on Friday night and Saturday when people had the time to get into trouble. I think Mr. Torelli would have been happier living in some place like New York City, where the crime is more frequent and more serious.

"Did you see the paper?" Ross asked when I hooked up with him at his house.

"Which paper?"

"The *Beacon*." He gave me an odd look. "You didn't do an interview with Davis, did you?"

"What do you mean? Did *I* interview *him?*"

"No. Did he interview you?"

"No," I said. "Why would I — " Then I remembered our conversation on Friday. "Not really."

"Not really?"

I was starting to get impatient. "What's up, Ross?"

He turned his back to me. "It's in the front pocket of my backpack."

"What is?"

"The *Beacon*. Page five."

I unzipped the pocket, pulled out the paper and thumbed to page five.

The article wasn't long — it was one of three items that made up the weekly crime roundup. This particular one had Davis Kaye's byline.

Vandalism Hits East Hastings High

by Davis Kaye

The rear driver's-side tire of a blue Toyota owned by substitute teacher Allan Green was punctured while it sat in the East Hastings Regional High School parking lot last Thursday in what police say was a deliberate act of vandalism. The police began an investigation following a formal complaint by Mr. Green, who believes that the culprit is a student. There have been reports that a student was seen near Mr. Green's car the day of the incident.

I stopped reading and looked at Ross. "You have to be kidding. *A* student? How about *hundreds* of students? *This* is reporting?"

"Keep reading," he said.

Many students at East Hastings Regional told the Beacon *that it is no mystery who punctured the tire. Students have been openly congratulating one of their own for perpetrating the act of vandalism. When informed of this by a reporter for the* Beacon, *the student, who cannot be named because no charges have yet been laid, said,*

"You have no idea what that means to me."
Mr. Green, a resident of Elder Bay, is sub-
stituting for Gerald Lawry, who was injured
in a car accident ten days ago.

"You were being sarcastic, right?" Ross said.

I re-read the article, then crumpled the newspaper.

"Hey!" Ross said. "I haven't finished reading that!"

I shoved the balled-up paper into his hand.

"That isn't journalism," I said. "Hasn't anyone heard of ethics up here? This reads like the *Star*."

"It doesn't surprise me that Davis would write something like that," Ross said. "But I'm a little surprised that Mr. Torelli would run it."

"Not me," I said. "A backwater like this — if it weren't for this phony wannabe journalism, there'd be no journalism at all!"

"Hey!" Ross said. He looked as if he'd been slapped. But if he thought I was going to apologize for insulting his rinky-dink hometown, he was mistaken.

I don't think anyone else at school had read the *Beacon*. Nobody said anything. I got no peculiar looks from anyone. Nobody was whispering behind my back. Maybe, I thought, just maybe, my day would pass uneventfully.

Yeah. Right.

* * *

I had history right after homeroom. Mr. Green wasn't there when I entered the class. I allowed myself to hope that he was home nursing some non-trivial ailment. I glanced at his desk as I headed for mine and saw a newspaper neatly folded in the center of it. It was a copy of the *Beacon*, open to the page that contained Davis's so-called news item. Who had left it there? I scanned the room, but didn't see Davis. Sarah Moran was at her desk, her head bowed over a book. Rick and Brad were sprawled on their chairs, laughing about something. Me, perhaps? Daria, for once, looked directly at me. Her expression was impossible to read. But when I reached out to grab the newspaper from Mr. Green's desk, her eyes shifted to the door. A warning? From Daria? Not likely. But her look made me turn and I saw Mr. Green frowning at me. No wonder — my hand was poised over the newspaper. I should have grabbed it and run. But where? Mr. Green was not only blocking the exit, he was also closing in on me fast. I retreated to my desk. Here we go again, I thought.

Mr. Green set his briefcase onto his desk. He opened it and pulled out his textbook and notes. Then he closed the case and stood it behind the desk. I watched his every move. He set the textbook on top of the neatly folded newspaper. With any luck, it would stay there, concealing the article.

If luck had been a student in Mr. Green's history class, it would have been marked absent that day. Mr. Green sat down. He opened his textbook. He tilted his head and seemed to notice the newspaper. Frowning, he pulled it out and studied it.

Splotches appeared first on his neck, then on his cheeks. Without looking up, he slipped the newspaper back under his textbook. When the bell rang, he stood up and began his lesson. He didn't look at me even once. At first I was relieved. Then it dawned on me — he was ignoring me. Part of me was grateful. The rest of me felt sort of sick. The knot in my stomach told me that things were going to get worse before they got better.

Finally the bell rang, freeing me from Mr. Green's classroom. I passed the office on my way from history to math. As I did, I spotted Steve Denby standing at the counter. He didn't see me, but I had the feeling that his presence wasn't accidental.

At lunchtime I went down to the newspaper office. Ross said, "I saw Davis talking to the police."

"Oh?"

"You think it was about that article in the *Beacon*?"

"How am I supposed to know that, Ross?" I guess you could say I almost bit off his head. He didn't say anything else to me.

After school I reported for the last day of my five-day detention. I took a seat in the classroom that doubled as the detention hall, and waited. It looked like I was going to be the only customer. Then Dean Abbott stumbled into the room, took a seat in the back row and opened a magazine. The bell rang. Mr. Green came in, carrying two large books.

"Right," he said, even though neither Dean nor I

had said a word. "Both of you, come here and take one of these." He was holding up two copies of the *Oxford Canadian Dictionary*.

"Now, open them up to a page."

I looked blankly at him.

"Which page?" Dean said.

"For Pete's sake," Mr. Green said. He grabbed my dictionary, even though I wasn't the one who had asked the question, opened it at random, and thrust it back at me. Then he glowered at Dean, who shrugged and opened his own copy.

"You go to the front chalkboard," he said to me. To Dean, "You take the side board. Start at the top left-hand page. Copy out each word, followed by its definition. Then use the word in a sentence. A real sentence. If, for example, the word is *incongruous*, you are *not* to write, *It was incongruous*. You are to write a sentence that clearly demonstrates your grasp of the word."

I glanced at Dean, who was doing a pretty good imitation of a guy trying to decipher a set of instructions that was not being communicated in any language he had ever encountered. I would have been willing to bet that *incongruous* wasn't in his vocabulary.

"Go!" Mr. Green commanded.

We went to our chalkboards. The first entry on my page was *shipping lane*. I took it from there, writing fast and thinking that Mr. Green was a real jerk. But, hey, if an improved vocabulary was the extent of my punishment, I could take it. I moved along quickly through *shipwright, shirt* and *shish kebab*. Then I was brought up short by the next word.

"Um, Mr. Green?" I said.

"No talking," he said.

"But, sir — "

"Ms. Yan, this detention is not about talking. It's about atoning. Do as you were told."

Well, okay then. I passed on to the next word. Who said detentions are all work and no play? Then came the next word and the next word. I heard a strangled sound from the side of the classroom. I glanced over at Dean, who was biting his knuckles to stifle what threatened to be an explosion of laughter. At least someone was enjoying my work.

I was nearly at the bottom of the page when the bell rang. Mr. Green dismissed us. I was gathering up my things when he turned to look at what I had written. Red splotches appeared on his neck. I managed to keep a straight face.

"I will see you tomorrow after school," Mr. Green said to me.

"My detention is finished," I pointed out. "This was my last day."

He was spluttering as he looked from me to the chalkboard and back again.

"I was just following your instructions," I said. "I have a witness, right, Dean?"

Dean's nod was swift and eager.

Mr. Green wasn't paying attention. He had grabbed an eraser and was undoing all my hard work.

* * *

I was on my way out of school when I saw Davis heading for the main exit.

"Hey!" I yelled. He turned and looked at me. If he sensed my anger, it didn't show. In fact, it seemed to take him a moment to register that I was talking to him. I guess he had more important things on his mind.

"What's the matter with you?" I demanded. "Didn't they teach you anything in that snotty private school of yours?"

He managed to look both innocent and perplexed. "I was on the honor roll," he said. "They taught me a lot. For example, a police officer called me into the office today and asked me to divulge my source."

Steve Denby. Geez.

"I didn't tell him." He smiled at me.

If he was waiting for me to thank him, he'd have to wait himself into the grave.

"They obviously didn't teach you about ethics," I said.

One thin, blond eyebrow arched.

"That so-called article of yours in the *Beacon* is nothing but innuendo," I said. "Innuendo that makes me look guilty of something."

The eyebrow crept higher.

"Oh?" he said. "I don't recall mentioning your name."

"You quoted me."

"Did I?"

"'You have no idea what that means to me.' I said that to you last Friday when you were trying to get information out of me. In case no one has mentioned this to you before," I said, "it's wrong, wrong and — did I mention this? — *wrong,* to quote someone without saying who you're quoting."

"Uh-huh," Davis said. "That would account for all those 'an inside source said' stories you see in the newspaper all the time."

"Second," I said, "you got it all wrong."

"You just finished telling me that you said it."

"When I said it, I was being sarcastic. I didn't touch Mr. Green's car."

His other eyebrow crept up his forehead. "You were being *sarcastic?* Then how come when I talked to eleven different people who said that they'd congratulated you on what you did to Mr. Green's tire, none of them told me that you had denied doing it? What's going on, Chloe? Were you trying to make yourself out to be a hero around here by taking credit for something you didn't do? Or did you really do it, but now that everyone knows, you're too cowardly to admit it?"

I wish I could say I don't know what came over me. I wish I could say I was shocked by what I did next. But I do know what came over me — rage. And I wasn't shocked because the truth is, every now and again, I lose it — *it* being my temper. I thrust out my hands and shoved Davis so hard that he reeled backward and slammed against one of the trophy display cases that ran along both sides of the school entrance. Fortunately he hit wood, not glass, so nothing shattered. But I heard a *whoomph* as the air was knocked out of his lungs. His knees buckled. For a moment it threatened to turn into one of those cartoon moves. You know, where one character hits another character and the character who was hit hangs in the air for a moment before suddenly crumpling into a heap on the ground. But Davis didn't crumple. He looked at me, stunned. Then he struggled to a standing position and said, "You don't make things easy on yourself, do you?"

That's when I knew he was going to report me. I wasn't going to beg him not to, though. I wasn't going to give him any more reasons to gloat. I watched him straighten his jacket and sling his pack over one shoulder. Then I watched him stride down the hall in the general direction of the office. Only then did I look around and see that we had not been alone. Someone had been watching the whole time. That someone was Daria Dattillo.

Chapter 7

I admit it, I was completely pathetic. I had piles of homework, but instead of tackling it, I hovered around the front door waiting for Levesque. I had stopped by the police station on the way home, but he wasn't there. I wondered if Ms. Jeffries had already called him. I hoped not. If he had to hear one more piece of bad news about me, I wanted him to hear it from me first. That way at least I wouldn't come across as the coward Davis was making me out to be. I'd be a straight-shooter. *Look at me, I'm not hiding in my room, I'm doing the right thing, I'm stepping forward and confessing what I did. Pick your punishment. I deserve it. I deserve it all. Just spare me your disappointment.* It wasn't even much of a break that Mom was out of town. She called every night to talk to Phoebe and me, and usually called again later to talk to Levesque. If I didn't tell her what had happened, Levesque would.

It was a little after eight when I heard the gun-fire sound of gravel under the wheels of his car as he came up the driveway. Everything sounded louder to me in the country than it did in the city. This was especially true at night. I'm not sure why that is, but it is. One car on gravel sounded like ten. Two loons calling on the lake sound like twenty. I heard Levesque's car engine hum, then die. I heard his car door open, then *thunk* shut. I heard a key in the front door. I heard the front door open and close again. And I waited. I waited until he had his boots off and his slippers on before I said, "Did you happen to talk to Ms. Jeffries today?"

His eyes zeroed in on me.

"About what?"

"About me." Technically, I was a who, not a what.

His expression didn't change, but I heard a little "what-now?" sigh seep from him.

"It's not like I'm *trying* to get into trouble," I said.

"Sometimes I wonder how hard you're trying to stay out of it."

His words were like a match being held to the fuse of my temper. I had to struggle to blow it out.

"There's a guy who's been giving me a hard time," I said. "The same guy who wrote an article in the *Beacon* about what happened to Mr. Green's car."

He nodded, which meant he knew what I was talking about. That made sense. If Steve Denby had been at school today talking to Davis, it was because Levesque had sent him.

"I guess you could say I shoved the guy," I said.

"You *guess* I could say that?"

"Okay, so I did it. I shoved him."

"Did you hurt him?"

"He walked away, if that's what you mean."

The look he gave me made it clear that wasn't what he meant.

"Maybe he's going to have a bruise on his back," I said. "But he walked away and he wasn't limping or anything. And nothing got broken."

Levesque shook his head.

"You're on pretty thin ice at school right now," he said. "I would have thought you'd be a little more circumspect."

Gee, what had happened to his unshakable belief in me?

"I didn't touch Mr. Green's car," I said.

"Yet there's a widespread impression in your school that you did. And from what I've heard, you've done nothing to dispel that impression. Quite the opposite, in fact. You've actually taken credit for what happened."

"It's not my fault that people don't like Mr. Green," I said. "They kept congratulating me. They wouldn't listen when I said I didn't do it. After a while, I just decided to let it ride."

"That's rarely a good idea," he said.

"I didn't do anything wrong," I said. My voice sounded shrill.

"You just said you pushed a boy."

"He provoked me."

Levesque shook his head again. "You have to keep your head, Chloe," he said. "When people think things that aren't true, and when what they think could land you in big trouble, you have to keep your head."

"Thanks," I muttered. "I'll try to remember that."

When Mom called, she asked me how I was. I said I was fine. Then she told me how well Brynn was doing at school. Rah-rah, Brynn. She didn't grill me and I didn't tell her what was happening around here. I decided to leave that to Levesque. I didn't want to hassle with it anymore.

* * *

"How's your cafeteria story going?" Ross asked, as we walked to school together the next morning.

"It's going."

"You have a deadline, you know," Ross said.

"It'll be done on time," I said. Never mind that I was probably going to get hauled down to the office again today. Never mind that I'd be phenomenally lucky if all I got was a detention this time. Never mind that I was probably looking at a suspension. And especially never mind that, this time, Levesque wasn't taking my side.

Ross stopped bugging me about the story and my deadline when we got to school. As he did every Tuesday morning, he headed directly for the boxes that sit just inside the front door. The *Herald* was delivered to school on Tuesday and Ross always grabbed a copy and read every word to assure himself that it was perfect — if it was. Sometimes a few typos crept in. That drove him crazy.

I glanced at the paper. The reader survey was in it. I spent about two seconds wondering how many people would fill it in and drop it in the box Ross had set up on the counter inside the *Herald* office. Then I went right back to wondering when I would get called to the office.

Homeroom passed and nothing happened.

First period passed, then second period, and I was still not summoned by Ms. Jeffries. Then something worse happened.

Ms. Peters handed out our new assignments. We were given a book or a play — her choice, right down to the title; Ms. Peters is a control freak — which we were supposed to analyze with respect to the social issues it raised. I got *Spartacus*. Oh, and I got a partner. Everyone did. Chosen by Ms. Peters. I got Davis Kaye. He showed no reaction to this news one way or the other. When I glanced at him to check, he was staring at his desk. He looked like he hadn't slept in a month. Poor Davis.

"Ms. Peters?" I said. I had waited for the classroom to clear before approaching her. "Can I talk to you about the assignment?"

She glanced up from the paper she was reading.

"Problem?" she said.

"I was just wondering if there's any way I could switch partners."

She looked at me as if I had asked to switch heads with her.

"The assignments have been made," she said.

"I know, but if I could arrange to change partners with someone, would that be okay?"

"Do you have a problem with . . . " She ran her

finger down a sheet of paper, her list of assignments, I realized. "With Davis?" she said.

"Well, as a matter of fact — "

"Because if you do, I'm afraid you're just going to have to work it out. Part of this assignment is about academic learning," she said. "Part of it is about life skills, which are just as important. You'll find that once you've graduated and are out in the real world, you'll be called upon to work with all kinds of people."

Gosh, do you think?

"Often you won't have a choice," she said. "You have to learn to get along with all types of people. Whatever differences you have with Davis, I'm sure you'll find a way to work them out and get this assignment done."

I didn't waste any more breath arguing with her. I had tried it in the past and had never won. Given how my life had been going recently, there was no reason to think that was going to change any time soon.

I left the classroom and ran smack into Davis, which wasn't hard because he was leaning against a bank of lockers right outside the door.

"I don't care if you heard that," I informed him.

He looked a little dazed. "Heard what?"

"Nice act," I said.

Now he looked confused. "I just wanted to talk to you about — "

"If we have to be partners, we have to be partners," I said. He blinked at me like I was the sun and he was a creature who had just crawled out from a lifetime under a rock. "Start reading the book and meet me in the library after school tomorrow so we can divide up the work. I'm not doing this alone and I'm not getting less than an A. Understand?"

He nodded. He opened his mouth and I braced myself for some Davis boasting — he'd probably won awards for social analysis at his old school. But he didn't say anything. He was acting very un-Davis-like. I decided that I liked the change. Only after I left him did I remember that he had wanted to talk to me. Too bad for him.

I went to the newspaper office after school, plunked myself down in front of a free computer and banged out my cafeteria story. Then I printed it and slapped it on Ross's desk. He looked up at me in surprise.

"Problem?" he said.

"I hate football," I said.

"Hey!" said Eric, glancing up from his computer, where he was probably composing an ode to the sport.

"Hey what?" I said. "It attracts Neanderthals."

"It attracts warrior athletes," he said, without missing a beat. I wondered how often he'd said that or how long he'd been saving it up, waiting for the opportunity to slide it into a conversation.

"Neanderthals," I repeated, "who come fully equipped with massive egos, bad senses of humor, complete disdain for anyone who doesn't play their sport, oh, and did I mention this, massive egos."

"Which Huskie bit you?" Eric asked. The East Hastings High football team was called the Huskies — don't ask me why, we're not that far north. Then he and Ross exchanged a knowing look.

"What?" I said.

"What what?" Eric said.

"That look. What is that?"

"Nothing," Ross said.

Right. "Liar."

"Everybody knows about what happened between you and Rick," Eric said. "He makes cracks about you in the locker room."

"Yeah, well, I guess *everybody* took that into consideration when he gave me this assignment." I glowered at Ross.

Ross scanned my story. "Didn't enjoy it, huh?"

"Hated it," I said. "I'm going home."

Ross shut off his computer. "Me, too," he said. "I'll come with you."

While we walked, I spilled out all my football hostility. About ninety-nine percent of it was directed at Rick.

"Sounds like you wouldn't be so down on the sport if you hadn't been dumb enough to go out with Rick."

"Thanks."

"Hey, look on the bright side, the way he's going, he's not likely to be in any of your classes next year. As to your ability to say no — " He shrugged.

I left Ross at the foot of his driveway and headed up to the park. The place was like a magnet to me. Sometimes when I walked through it, listening to birds calling to each other, turning at the scuffle of a chipmunk or a squirrel in the dry leaves that littered the ground, inhaling the fragrance of cedar and pine, my eyes filled with dozens of hues of green from pine needles and beech leaves and oak leaves and ferns and moss, I felt . . . well . . . happy. And at times like that, the citified life I had led until recently faded into a wash of gray.

I smiled to myself — I really did — as I cut through the woods on the north side of Lodge Lake Road and headed for the road that ringed Little Lodge Lake. At more or less regular intervals, driveways cut off the road, leading to lakeside cottages. Must be nice, I thought, to wake up every morning and look out at shimmering water. I strolled along, thinking about lakes and swimming and the end of the school year and whether I was going to be able to find a summer job. I would have strolled along until lake gave way to park and park gave way to railway lands and then, next thing I knew, I'd be home, if something hadn't glinted in the sun, catching my eye. I turned to look.

Something on a gravel driveway was giving off a blinding light. I walked a little way up the driveway and corrected myself. Something there had caught the sun and was reflecting it back into my eyes. The culprit was a pair of sunglasses. I ducked down and picked them up. They had expensive-looking designer frames. They'd probably been dropped by whoever owned the cottage. I could leave them where they were and hope whoever had dropped them didn't drive over them next time he or she went into town. I could move them to the side of the driveway where they'd be safe, but wouldn't necessarily be easily found. Or I could do the neighborly thing and march right up to the house and return them. It was a beautiful afternoon and I was feeling downright neighborly.

I hiked up the gravel driveway that cut through a tight grove of pine. It was a minute before the cottage came in sight, and when it did I saw what I assumed was a sign of life — the front door was open. It wasn't until I got close to the paving stones that cut through the grass from the driveway to the cottage that I started to feel that something was wrong.

For one thing, it was quiet. Too quiet. When the door to a house or cottage is open like that, you expect someone to eventually bustle in or out. Neither happened. Nor did I hear any people sounds — footsteps, a radio or TV playing, work noises. Still, some people are quiet, so maybe that wasn't a big deal. Then I saw splotches of — what? Paint maybe. They started at the front door — or maybe they started inside the cottage, I don't know — came down the steps, and ran along the paving stones and over to the garage that stood at the head of the driveway. Had someone spilled something?

"Hello?" I called.

No answer. It occurred to me then that maybe I had stumbled onto another cottage break-in. I approached the door, sidestepping the splotches, and cautiously peered inside.

"Hello?" I called again.

Still no answer.

I turned and looked down at the trail of splotches. By now I had a weird feeling. I followed the trail to the garage.

"Hello?" I called.

The main garage doors were closed, but the small side door stood open. Something had been smeared onto the doorknob. Something dark-brownish. I wasn't sure what it was and I didn't touch it. I poked my head through the door and saw a car — a cream-colored Jaguar. I blinked in the dim garage light and saw that there was someone inside. Someone who was slumped sideways in the front seat. Someone who wasn't moving.

Stay out of there, a voice in my head said. Stay out and call someone. Call Levesque.

Sensible, right?

I used to groan when the main character in a horror movie heard a noise, say, down in the basement or up in the attic and, instead of running as fast as possible in the opposite direction, he or she would light a candle (the easier to be left completely in the dark when something inevitably blew it out) and head directly for the sound. I don't think I'll ever groan again. Because now I get it. I get why they don't do what you'd think they *logically* should do. It's something in the air. Disaster or doom or fate — whatever you want to call it — sends out a powerful signal that human beings, cursed with curiosity, cannot ignore.

Someone was slumped in the front seat of the car. That someone wasn't moving. I recognized the car. It was the one I had seen on the side of the road near the park on Friday. Those facts worked on me like a magnet on iron. I found myself drawn into the garage, drawn to the car, drawn to bend down and peer through the window. Then I was fixed there, even when every nerve ending in my body told me to run, run now, run fast and run far, even when my stomach churned and I knew that whatever was in it was coming up, fast and soon.

The man slumped in the front seat was the same man I had seen in the phone booth outside the park a few days ago, the one who had yelled at me and scared me off. The front of his shirt was soaked in something dark-brownish. It didn't take advanced training in forensic science to know that it was blood. His hand was stretched out — toward the cell phone in the holder attached to the dashboard. His eyes were open. His mouth sagged. Nothing moved.

It may have taken me a split second to digest these facts. It may have taken me five minutes. I don't know. I ducked. I looked. I processed the information. Then and only then did I back out of the garage. Then and only then did I throw up on

85

the grass between the garage and the house. Then and only then did I remember the good advice I had already given myself. Call someone. Call Levesque.

Phone. Phoebe had a cell phone. She took as many baby-sitting jobs as she could get to pay for it. I didn't have one, hadn't wanted one. In a town this size, you see everyone every day. Sometimes more times a day than you wanted to. Mostly I was trying for privacy, not for more contact with the citizens of East Hastings. Right now, though, I would have given every dollar I had, and my right arm, for a cell phone. There was one in the car, but I knew enough not to touch that, not to touch anything, not even the car itself. I spun around as if I expected to find a phone right beside the garage. Nothing. Maybe there was one in the cottage. If there was, I wasn't going in to look for it. I wasn't going to cross that splotchy trail. I wasn't going to mess up a crime scene.

Think, Chloe. Where was the nearest phone? A neighboring cottage? Most of them were empty this time of year. The nearest phone was . . . the pay phone near the entrance to the park.

I ran, still holding the pair of sunglasses I had picked up from the driveway.

I ran until I thought my lungs would burst. I think everything that had been in my backpack ended up on the ground around the phone booth as I hunted for a quarter. I found one. My fingers trembled as I pushed it into the slot and punched in numbers. Only then did it occur to me that I could have dialed 911 without a coin. Still, I thought I was pretty much in control as I waited for someone to pick up.

"Police Department. Levesque speaking."

I thought I was calmly reporting what I had seen. I was sure that I was speaking slowly and clearly.

"Slow down, Chloe," Levesque said. "Take a deep breath." Then, when I kept right on talking, "Chloe," he commanded, "stop talking and take a deep breath."

I obeyed.

"Where are you?" he said.

I told him. Then I said, "I think he's dead, but I'm not sure. I'm not sure."

He told me to stay where I was. He told me to sit down out of the way of traffic and to stay put until he came and got me. I promised I would.

Chapter 8

I was standing in the phone booth, staring at the sunglasses that I had set down next to the phone, when an East Hastings police car pulled up in front of the booth and Levesque got out.

I dropped the receiver back into its cradle.

"You okay?" Levesque asked. He was peering at me, assessing me.

"Not so much," I admitted.

"Get in the car," he said. "I'm going to have to stop by there before I take you home, okay?"

"Okay."

In a couple of minutes Levesque turned into the long driveway. The gravel popped under our wheels as we approached the two other cars that had arrived since I was last there. One was a police car. I didn't recognize the other one. Steve Denby was standing well away from the garage with a woman. She was holding a black medical bag. When he turned toward us, I saw that he looked pale too. I guess Steve was like me. I guess he hadn't seen many dead people either.

"Stay in the car, okay?" Levesque said.

No problem. I didn't want to look at that garage again, let alone go near it.

Levesque got out of the car and walked over to Steve and the woman. They talked for a few minutes, then Steve went back to his car and opened the trunk. Levesque disappeared into the garage. It seemed to me that he was in there for a long time. When he finally came out he stopped and spoke to Steve again. Then he came back to the car, got in behind the wheel and turned to me.

"How did you happen to find him?" he asked.

I handed him the sunglasses and told him how they had led me up the driveway to the cottage. Once I started talking, I couldn't stop. I told him about seeing the man before, in the same phone booth I had just called from. Then I started to shake all over. A couple of days ago, the guy had been a living, breathing old grump who had chased me angrily from his car. Today he was dead.

"I'm going to drive you home," Levesque said. His voice was soft. He peered into my eyes. "Then I have to come back here. Okay?"

I nodded.

"You're not to say anything to anybody about this, understand? Not that you found him. Not where you found him. Not what you saw. Nothing, you understand?"

I nodded again.

"Maybe if I'd passed by here earlier," I said. "Maybe he would have been alive. Maybe I could have — "

"You'd have had to pass by some time this morning," Levesque said. "It looks like he's been dead at least eight or nine hours. There's nothing you could have done."

He dropped me off in front of our house, asked me once again if I was sure I was okay, and then headed back to the crime scene.

Phoebe was doing her homework up in her room by the time I got home. I decided not to bother her. I thought about all the assignments hanging over my head — my English project, my history essay. If I were smart, I'd do exactly what my little sister was doing. I staked out the dining room table, opened my books . . . and accomplished exactly nothing. A man was dead. I was pretty sure now that those splotches on the steps, the path and the driveway were blood. He had died violently and, unless it was suicide, someone had killed him. I'm no expert, but suicide didn't seem likely, not from what I've heard and seen on TV about the subject. Suicides involving lots of blood are usually shootings. The man looked like he had been shot in the chest. People who shoot themselves usually aim higher. If he'd shot himself where suicides usually shoot themselves, I don't think I'd have been able to recognize him. I started to shiver all over.

Levesque called at ten o'clock to ask how I was. I said I was fine. I felt fine too — except that I couldn't shake the picture of the dead man that appeared every time I closed my eyes. Levesque said he would be home late. In fact, he came home early — early the next morning. He walked through the front door while I was pouring my first cup of coffee. I handed my mug to him and poured myself another.

"You okay?" he asked.

I nodded. "Mom called," I said. "Twice. She wants you to call her."

He glanced at the clock. It was only seven-thirty. Then he gulped down some coffee.

"Can I ask you something?" I said.

He didn't say no.

"Who was he? You know, the dead guy."

"His name was Stanley Meadows," Levesque said. He sank down at the kitchen table. His face was gray. He needed a shave. The knees of his pants were crusted with dirt.

"Was he murdered?"

He gave me a weary look. I knew exactly what he was thinking: *Do I have to deliver my lecture again?* The lecture was about official police business being out of bounds to civilians.

"Aw, come on," I said. "I found the guy. I dreamed about him all night." That dream had been a nightmare.

"You can't — "

" — tell anyone," I said. "I know."

He hesitated for so long that I thought he was going to stick to his rules. Then he said. "It looks like someone broke into the cottage. A window around the back had been pried open."

"Another break and enter?" That's just what I'd

91

thought after I saw that the front door was open.

"Could be."

"So someone broke in not knowing Meadows was there, and he surprised them and they killed him, right?"

"It's a theory," he said.

"What do you mean, it's a theory?" I asked. "His place was broken into, just like those other places."

"I like to keep an open mind."

"What about the sunglasses? Do you think the killer dropped them?"

"Don't know yet," he said.

Something else was bothering me.

"If he surprised someone breaking into his place, then he was probably shot in the house, right?" I said. The blood spatters ran from the front door, along the walk, to the garage. "So, if he was shot in his house, what was he doing in his car?"

"There's no phone in the cottage," Levesque said. "My guess is he left his cell phone in the car and he went out there to call for help."

I shuddered as I thought of Stanley Meadows slumped on the buttery leather upholstery of his cream-colored car, too weak to make that call.

"Now what?" I said.

"Now I'm going to catch a few hours of sleep. Then I have to go back to work. I don't know when I'm going to be home. Will you and Phoebe be okay?"

I gave him a sour look. Eighteen months ago when we still lived in Montreal and Mom was still a waitress, my sisters and I had pretty much looked after ourselves. Did he think we'd forgotten how to do that?

* * *

"Did you hear the news?" Ross said. Then, "Stupid question. Do they have any idea what happened?"

"You've met Levesque, right?" I said.

"Yeah," he said, looking puzzled. "Why?"

"It was a rhetorical question, Ross. Think about it."

He didn't have to think for long. "It's kinda like having a secret agent for a father, isn't it?" he said.

"Well, I wouldn't know, Ross. Levesque's not a secret agent." I didn't mention that I was the one who had found the body. Levesque had told me not to. Just as well. If I volunteered that piece of information, dozens of people would start pumping me for details.

I had trouble concentrating that morning. I hadn't slept well and the more I tried not to think about Stanley Meadows, the more he occupied my mind. So did the dark stains I had seen on the front steps and the walkway. The guy had been bleeding. He had been trying to get to the one phone on the property, the cell phone in his car, so that he could call for help. He hadn't made it. Even though I didn't know Stanley Meadows — and my only encounter with him had left me with a less than favorable impression — I felt bad for him. I wondered if he was married or had kids. If so, had they been located? Had someone given them the bad news? How had they reacted? Those thoughts kept rattling around in my head when I was supposed to be doing schoolwork. So at lunch, I decided to get some air.

I headed out a back door and, whoa, what do you know, there was Sarah, wrapped around Davis like paper on a Christmas package. She was smaller than Davis. His chin was resting on her head. He seemed to be staring out into space. I turned and scooted around the side of the school. There are some things I'm not interested in witnessing.

I thought I'd head down to Pine Lake and walk its sandy beach. At this time of year, there are never many people on it. I was cutting across the school parking lot when I saw that the rear passenger door of one of the cars was open. There was no one around. I figured someone must have left the door open by mistake. I decided to close it. That'll teach me. When I reached in to push down the lock button, that's when I noticed that the small rear window was broken. Pebbles of glass littered the seat and the carpet on the floor inside. A piece of paper lay on the floor. I started to reach for it, but a voice in my head said, don't touch anything. I was backing away from the car when I heard another voice. This one was yelling at me. I turned and looked back at the school. Mr. Green was standing at a window on the second floor, shouting at me to stay where I was. I backed up a pace. Mr. Green's face disappeared from the window. Two or three minutes later, he raced out of the school. He was gasping for breath when he reached me. For a young guy, Mr. Green wasn't in good shape. Too much time with his nose in a history book, I guess.

He grabbed me by the arm and held tight as he inspected the car. *His* car, I now realized. There seemed to be no limit to how stupid Mr. Green thought I was. He had seen me touching his car. He had as much announced this from a second-floor window. What good would it have done me to run away? Even if I *had* decided to make myself scarce, I'd have done it between the time he was at the window and the time he came out of the school, not now.

Mr. Green picked up the piece of paper. He studied it a moment before glowering at me.

"Where is it?" he said

"Where's what?"

"You're going to pay for this."

"I didn't do anything," I said. Boy, those were four words I was getting tired of saying.

"Is that right?" he said. "Then explain this."

He thrust the paper at me. It was a photocopy of a page from the *Oxford Canadian Dictionary*. The first entry on the page was *shipping lane*. Someone was working overtime to give me a lot of grief.

"We're going to the office," he said. "Right now."

Mr. Green must have learned something from the punctured-tire incident because this time he didn't touch anything except me. He started to march me to the office. I was angry — at him because I hadn't done anything, but knew he would never believe me — and at whoever had vandalized his car — *again* — and had pointed yet another finger at me.

Mr. Green must have attracted a lot of attention on his way out of the school to nab me because by the time he hauled me back inside, a crowd had gathered. I heard someone say something about Mr. Green's car, but I didn't see who it was. A lot of people were whispering.

Ms. Jeffries glanced through the wall of glass that separated her office from the main administration office. She got up slowly, shaking her head. She reminded me of my mom whenever she caught me tormenting Phoebe, *again*. Her expression said, how many times are you planning to disappoint me, Chloe? Before Ms. Jeffries reached us, Mr. Green was proclaiming that he had caught me breaking into his car. The next thing I knew, I was occupying what was fast becoming *my* chair in Ms. Jeffries's office. Mr. Green told his side of the story, then Ms. Jeffries looked expectantly at me.

"Well, Chloe?" she said.

"Well, what? He didn't catch me breaking into his car. He saw me *near* his car and he *assumed* that I did it."

"One of the windows was broken," Mr. Green said.

"I didn't break it."

"A very important file is missing."

I felt like asking why he'd left it in his car if it

was so important, but that probably would have made things worse, not better.

"Why don't you call the police?" I said. "They can even fingerprint me."

"That would be as useful as calling in a fox to do a head count in the henhouse, wouldn't it?" Mr. Green said.

"Hey!" I said. He could say what he wanted about me, but there was no way I was going to let him insult Levesque or suggest that Levesque would play favorites.

Ms. Jeffries sighed. "I'll take it from here if you don't mind, Mr. Green." Her weary voice matched her tired face.

Mr. Green seemed startled to find himself dismissed, but he got up and left the office. Ms. Jeffries leaned back in her chair and sighed again.

"What's going on, Chloe?" she asked. "You don't strike me as the kind of girl who cheats on tests and breaks into cars."

I told her exactly what had happened in the parking lot. She peered into my eyes while I spoke, looking for something. The truth, I think.

"The incident is going to have to be reported," she said.

I nodded.

"Maybe if you could just stay out of the parking lot . . . " she said.

I had a better idea. I was going to put a stop to whoever was framing me. Someone — besides me — was going to pay.

Chapter 9

It was turning out to be like one of those gang killings in a crowded nightclub. There's a couple of hundred people in the place, someone is shot, but when the police start asking questions, it turns out that those couple of hundred people were all in the bathroom when it happened. In other words, no one saw anything. But everyone was giving me a hard time about getting caught red-handed as I was supposedly breaking into Mr. Green's car.

"See, the way it works," Rick said, "is that you're supposed to check first to make sure no one is looking."

Everyone was speculating about what had been in the stolen file folder.

"Next week's history test?" Rick guessed. "Or did you score really big? Was it the final exam?"

It didn't take long for me to get tired of all the buzzing. By the end of the day I wished that I had arranged to meet Davis somewhere far from school. The only consolation was that the school library was the one place in all of East Hastings where I was in no danger of running into Rick and his football buddies.

As it turned out, I wasn't in much danger of running into Davis, either. Half an hour after we were supposed to have met, he still wasn't there. My mood had been bad enough when I arrived at the library. By the time thirty Davis-free minutes had ticked by, I was steaming. If he thought I was going to do all the work on this assignment, he was going to have to think again. And if he thought he was going to make things worse for me with Ms. Peters by refusing to work with me, well, same thing.

I had no idea where Davis lived. I thought of dialing 411, but remembered that Davis and his mother were living with his grandmother, and I had no idea what her last name was. But I knew someone who might know.

Ross was in the newspaper office. There were times when he seemed to live there.

"Davis," I said, as I came through the door. "Where does he live?"

"Why?"

"Do you know or not, Ross?"

"Love your approach to coaxing information out of people," Ross said. "First you soften them up with your charm, then you pop the big question. Bet it works like magic every time."

"It works as well as your sarcasm," I said. "Davis was supposed to meet me at the library. He stood me up. And don't give me that look, Ross. He was supposed to meet me because Ms. Peters paired us up for an English assignment."

Ross grinned. "Things just aren't going your way lately, are they?"

"As long as I don't stumble across any *more* dead bodies, I think I can handle it," I shot back. "So, do you know where he lives?"

"What?"

For some reason, Ross had perked right up.

"Do you know where he lives?" I repeated, speaking a little louder and pausing between words so that he could easily digest each one.

"What do you mean, as long as you don't stumble across any more dead bodies? Are you talking about that guy they found dead up near Little Lodge Lake, that guy Meadows?"

Oops.

"It was just a figure of speech, Ross."

He didn't buy it, not that I expected him to. Ross can be a little naïve at times, but he's not stupid.

"*You* found the guy, didn't you?" he said. "What can you tell me about it?"

"Nothing," I said. "They're still investigating. Levesque would kill me."

"Tell me later? After it's over?"

"Do you have to sound so eager for the gory details?" I said. "It's kind of creepy. I mean, he was a body by the time I found him, not a person."

"I know where he lives."

"Davis?"

He nodded. "And he's not in the phone book." I waited, but Ross didn't volunteer the address.

"Okay, okay," I said. "Once the case is closed, I'll tell you. But if I get any more nightmares as a result of reliving the traumatic experience, you're going to be sorry."

"Fifteen Macdonald Avenue," he said. "North of Centre, a block from Lodge Lake Road."

"Thanks."

"I'm going to hold you to that promise."

I shuddered. "Whatever makes your inner ghoul happy," I said, as I headed for the door again.

"Hey!" Ross said.

"What?"

"I heard about the car thing."

"I was framed."

I explained to him exactly what had happened.

"But how could anyone know you'd be right beside Mr. Green's car when he looked out the window?" he said. "How could anyone predict you'd even be in the parking lot when you were?"

"They couldn't," I said. "It doesn't matter, though. That page from the dictionary pretty much nails me as the person who did it. At least, it does as far as Mr. Green is concerned."

"Yeah, but how many people know about that?"

"Are you kidding?" I said. "The whole school knows. Dean was in detention with me, remember? You just have to say the words *shipping lane* to him and he laughs so hard he almost wets himself."

"But why?" Ross said. "Why would anyone do that to you?"

Good question. If I could ace it the way I aced

history tests, I'd be well on my way to answering another excellent question: Who? Sure, I knew I wasn't at the top of everyone's playlist. And, sure, there were a few people who might even have said they found me annoying or snotty or even rude. But I hadn't seriously considered that anyone disliked me enough to set out deliberately to make me look guilty of things that I would never do in a million years.

I tried to put the thought out of my head as I headed for my locker to get my jacket. First things first. And the first thing was Davis. I went over what I would say to him. I decided to start with how inconsiderate it was to keep someone waiting for thirty minutes, then move into how I was not, repeat *not*, going to do this assignment all by myself. By this time the school was more or less deserted. There was only one person in the corridor where my locker was located. Sarah. Her locker was almost directly opposite mine. She was standing on tiptoes, reaching for something on the top shelf. Maybe she didn't notice me. Maybe she was ignoring me. Either way, I didn't care. I opened my locker, grabbed my jacket, and slammed the door shut again. As I was hooking my lock back into place, she gave a little shout. I turned just in time to see a pile of stuff cascade out of her locker. Loose papers flew all over the hall. I ducked to gather up some of them, an automatic Good Samaritan reflex. It was only when I turned to hand them over to her that I saw she had been crying.

"Are you okay, Sarah?" I asked.

She wiped angrily at her tears and took the papers from my hand. "I'm fine," she said, "not that it's any of your business."

In the seven months I'd been at East Hastings Regional, I had had a nodding, hi-how's-it-going, distant but non-antagonistic relationship with Sarah. Only recently had she become hostile to me.

"She's always been at the top of her class," Ross had told me at the end of last term when I had beaten her for that honor. "I don't think she knows how to handle being second best."

If you ask me, she was handling it badly.

"Why are you so mad at me?" I said.

She didn't answer. Instead she bent down to pick up the rest of the stuff that had fallen from her locker. More papers, a couple of notebooks, and something else. She grabbed it fast and turned her back on me, as if she were trying to prevent me from seeing what she was shoving into her backpack. Too late. I had already gotten a pretty good look.

"Nice pens," I said. I should know. They were the same kind that I used. Purple pens. My favorite kind. She had a four-pack of them. At least, it used to be a four-pack. One pen was missing.

I wanted to tell myself that it was a coincidence. Those pens were mass-produced. There were probably millions of them in use around the world at that exact moment. They were sold in at least three stores in East Hastings. So what if Sarah had a package of them? Except that none of the papers that I had retrieved from the floor for her was written in purple ink. Nor could I remember ever seeing Sarah with a purple pen in her hand — not that I ever paid a huge amount of attention to her writing habits.

"You like them?" Sarah said. "You can have them."

She threw the package at me, then slammed her locker door. While I watched her march down the hall away from me, I thought, come on, nobody could get so upset about a little academic competition that they'd set out to deliberately sink a person, could they?

Could they?

* * *

15 Macdonald Avenue was a big, old-fashioned brick house with gingerbread trim that needed a fresh coat of paint in the worst way. When I got closer I saw that the brickwork could stand some repair too. Then I thought, geez, listen to me. Since we moved up here, Mom had gotten into the habit of driving through all the little towns in the area to gawk at the big, rambling houses that have been standing for the better part of a century. She liked to joke that she was looking for the perfect house. Sometimes I went with her. She'd point out all the good and bad points of each house we passed: This one's got a great sunroom. The shingles on that one are worn out; if we bought it, we'd have to roof it.

Houses used to be pretty much interchangeable

to me. But I had learned to catalog their flaws just like Mom. Bottom line? 15 Macdonald Avenue leaned a little too much and had too much peeling paint to be the happy home of a certain former big-city, private-school kid. I wondered what kind of house Davis had lived in before he was moved up here. I wondered how much he missed his old neighborhood, his old school and his old friends. I had hated East Hastings for the first few months I was here and, to be honest, I was still looking forward to graduating high school and heading back to the city. Not Toronto, though. Montreal.

The slim woman who answered the doorbell was about the same age as my mother, but much better dressed. She looked sensational in narrow black slacks, a violet sweater and a pair of black leather boots that I would have killed for. A gold watch decorated one slender wrist. Her gold earrings looked heavy and expensive. I was willing to bet she hadn't bought them at the jewelry counter of the Bay up in Morrisville.

"May I help you?" she said. *May,* not *can.*

"Is Davis here?" I asked, after introducing myself.

I heard a *clump, clump, clump* behind her, then a shaky voice said, "Who's there?" An old woman appeared, leaning heavily on a walker.

"It's a friend of Davis's, Mother," the woman said. She turned back to me. "I'm afraid he's not here at the moment. May I ask him to call you when he returns?"

"A friend?" said the old woman, Davis's grandmother, I guess. She peered around her daughter at me. I have no idea how old she was, but if they were carding at the centenarian ball, she'd have passed easily. Her skin was papery white and crumpled. Her hair was as wispy as a bit of summer cloud. Deep lines cut into her face. They made her look sad. I knew she was sick; Davis had said so. I wondered how sick she was and whether she was expected to get better.

"Are you the reason he's never here?" the old woman said to me. Her tone was accusing.

"Mother, please," Davis's mom said. She looked apologetically at me.

"Could you tell him I came by?" I said. "He'll know what it's about."

"I'll tell him," his mother said.

* * *

Levesque was at the stove when I got home.

"I thought you'd still be at work," I said. "You know, cracking the big case."

Instead, he cracked an egg into a bowl and whisked it up.

"Your mother called," he said. "I'm thinking of driving down to Toronto on Friday to pick her up from the train. Work permitting. You want to come?"

"I dunno. I have a ton of homework. I'll be okay here alone."

Shendor rowfed.

"Alone with company," I amended. I bent down to scratch behind her ears. If she'd been a cat, she would have purred. As it was, she turned to jelly.

Levesque was dropping pieces of chicken one by one into the beaten egg and then fishing them out and dragging them through a little mound of flour. He was frowning.

"Anything you want me to do?" I asked.

He didn't answer.

"Should I grab the fire extinguisher and put out that stove fire?" I said.

No reaction. Well, that made it official — he was deep in thought, which meant that I was off the hook. I left him to his cooking. He was still frowning after Phoebe had set the table and we were sitting down to eat.

"What's the matter, Dad?" Phoebe said. Phoebe had started calling Levesque Dad the minute the wedding ceremony was over. My big sister Brynn called him Louis. I did, too, sometimes.

"He's thinking about that murder," I said.

Levesque laid his fork aside. "We're probably going to get a fair amount of media attention up here in the next day or so," he said.

"How come?" Phoebe said.

I waited.

Levesque looked at us for a moment. "You're going to read about it in the paper tomorrow anyway," he said, "so I might as well tell you. Stanley Meadows was supposed to testify in an important court case next week. He was up here supposedly staying out of harm's way."

"What kind of court case?"

"A case against his business partner. It's complicated, but basically it comes down to fraud on a massive scale. Meadows says that when he stumbled on it, his partner offered him a lot of money to keep his mouth shut. Meadows turned him down and went to the police instead."

"Is the partner going to get off now that this Stanley Meadows is dead?" Phoebe asked.

"Apparently it's going to be much more difficult to get a conviction," Levesque said.

"Kind of a tough break for the cops," I said. "A guy who's key to a major case ends up getting killed in a piddly, small-town break and enter. What are the chances?"

As soon as I said the words, Levesque's eyes zeroed in on me.

"I think you call that irony," Phoebe said.

Maybe. But who cared? Because suddenly the pieces were falling into place. Stanley Meadows, making a phone call from a phone booth when he had a cell phone sitting in his car only a few feet away. Stanley Meadows doing a major freak-out when he saw me peering into his car. Stanley Meadows, found dead in his car in the garage next to the cottage.

"I know — " I said, before Levesque shook his head. A small shake, barely noticeable. But it was there all the same, and it was serious. A warning shake.

"You know what?" Phoebe said. Then, "Pass the salad."

I passed the salad. Phoebe helped herself to seconds, then said, "You know what, Chloe?"

"Nothing."

Levesque kept his eyes on me a heartbeat longer, before reaching for the salad bowl. I had suddenly lost my appetite. I was thinking back to what he had said the day after I'd found Meadows, when I'd asked if he thought Meadows had surprised whoever had broken into his place and had been killed by them. *"It's a theory,"* he'd said, even though I had thought it was obvious what had happened. It's a theory. Now it all clicked into place.

I was jarred out of my thoughts by the crunch of car wheels on gravel. Someone was coming up our driveway. I started to get up. Levesque waved me back into my chair.

"It's probably Steve," he said. "He said he'd swing by here on his way home."

I heard Levesque open the front door. Then I heard the door close. He must have stepped out to talk to Steve. It was a good ten minutes before he came back inside. He was frowning again. This time he was frowning at me.

"Steve tells me that someone broke into a car at your school," he said.

"Oh?"

"Who?" Phoebe said. "What car?"

"A teacher's car," Levesque told her.

"Which teacher?"

"Mr. Green," I said. "And it wasn't me."

Levesque shook his head. "Apparently Mr. Green

thinks differently." He sank down onto his chair. "Apparently he claims he caught you in the act."

"I didn't do — "

Levesque held up his hand. "For the record, I don't consider you a suspect," he said. "But I wouldn't mind hearing the whole story — for the record."

I told him everything that had happened. He listened in silence. After I finished he said, "Sounds like you got off on the wrong foot with that man and it's been one misstep after another ever since."

"I don't think he's going to be happy until I'm behind bars," I said.

"I doubt it'll come to that. Steve's going to look into it, though. He may want to talk to you."

"Does Steve have any idea what was in the file folder that was taken?"

Levesque nodded. "It was the draft of an article Green has been working on. He says he was going to submit it to an academic journal. He says it's his only copy."

"He doesn't have it on his computer?"

"His computer crashed a week ago. The hard drive was completely fried. Fortunately, he had printed out the draft first. Unfortunately, he hadn't made a copy yet. He was going to use the school photocopier. He's pretty upset."

I wasn't feeling exactly cheery myself. Unless and until I found out who was setting me up to be Mr. Green's Number One Problem Student, my life was going to be a series of false accusations and undeserved punishments. That ate at me while I did the dishes after supper. Who was responsible for all my trouble?

Daria wasn't exactly my number one fan. Her dislike of me had been simmering for months. Had it finally started to boil? Had she finally decided to get back at me for the massive embarrassment she had suffered because of her plagiarism?

Her new quarterback boyfriend didn't like me much, either. But the forgery on the crib sheet was so good that I had even doubted myself for a few moments. And my handwriting has a smooth flow to it. It's nothing like the chicken scratching I've seen in Rick's notebooks or the loopy swirls in Daria's. I couldn't figure a big, burly football player for a master forger. Daria, on the other hand, was a possibility.

And then, of course, there was Sarah. She was downright hostile to me. She was also well-supplied with my trademark purple pens. And she was smart, practically the smartest kid in the whole school. Someone that smart could pull off a little forgery if she set her mind to it. But Sarah was such a straight arrow. If she wanted to make me look bad, would she really do it that way? Wouldn't it make more sense for her to try to show me up academically or, if she really wanted to get down and dirty, to sabotage an assignment I was working on?

Assignment. Grrrrrr. That raised the whole nasty subject of Davis. How dare he ditch me! How dare he think he could blow me off!

It was only when I was lying in bed later that night that I started thinking about Stanley Meadows again.

A guy scheduled to testify in court against his partner gets shot and killed when he surprises a burglar in his cottage. *It's a theory.* I remembered the sound of the gravel popping like firecrackers under the tires of the squad car as Levesque and I drove back to the cottage. I had heard that sound again this evening when Steve drove up our gravel driveway. It would have sounded even louder in the still of the night. Surely a burglar would have heard that sound. The driveway leading to Stanley Meadows's cottage was long and deep with gravel. Unless he was stone deaf, a thief who had broken in through a window at the back of the cottage would have heard that sound. He would have fled. Which meant that it had to have happened the other way around — Meadows had to have been *inside* the cottage when the burglar broke in. But wouldn't a burglar have to be pretty stupid to break into a cottage without checking to see if there was a car in the garage or the driveway? I was pretty sure that was what Levesque hadn't wanted me to say. It was also why he didn't want me to say anything about the case and about finding the body. The only people who knew where Meadows had been found were Levesque, Steve, the doctor Steve had called to the scene, and me. Levesque wanted to keep it that way. He wanted everybody to think that the police believed that Meadows was killed by a burglar, because everybody included whoever had done it. If the killer thought he had gotten away with it, that could make things easier for Levesque.

Chapter 10

Levesque was sitting at the kitchen table, frowning at the newspaper, when I left the house the next morning. The Toronto newspaper was delivered to our house every morning. Stanley Meadows had made page one, but just barely. The story ran for two, maybe three, inches on the front page, then continued near the back of the paper. I'd read it and learned nothing that I didn't already know.

I don't usually walk by the police station on the way to school, but I took that route the next morning. I checked to make sure that Levesque hadn't driven to work in the time it had taken me to walk into town. When I saw that his car wasn't parked outside, I went in.

Steve Denby sat his desk, sipping coffee and staring at a computer screen.

"Hi, Steve," I said.

He looked up and smiled. "Hi, Chloe," he said. Then, "He's not here."

"I know. Actually, I wanted to talk to you."

"Oh?"

"You're investigating the break-in of Mr. Green's car, right?"

"Yeah." He sounded guarded now, as if he were afraid I was going to pump him for top secret information.

As I approached his desk, I noticed a plastic bag with a sheet of paper inside. It was the photocopy of the dictionary page that had been found on Mr. Green's back seat.

"Mr. Green told you I did it, right?"

Steve hesitated before he nodded.

"Well, I didn't," I said.

That earned me another curt nod. I had seen that nod before and I knew exactly what it meant. Steve Denby was turning into a clone of Louis Levesque. That nod said maybe I was guilty of breaking into Mr. Green's car and maybe I wasn't. Steve was keeping an open mind. That was his job.

"Come on, Steve," I said. "You know me. Why would I break into a teacher's car? Why would I break into *anyone's* car?"

"I understand there have been certain, um, personality conflicts between you and Mr. Green."

"Big deal. There are certain personality conflicts between me and a lot of people," I said. Steve smiled. "Did you find anything that might tell you what happened or who did it?"

He didn't answer.

"Come on," I begged. "Do you have any idea what I've been going through this past week?" I filled him in on the whole Mr. Green story, most of which he'd already heard, but never from my perspective. "Someone is making me look bad," I said. "And because of everything that's happened, Mr. Green is out to get me."

"Chloe, I have to keep an open mind."

See what I mean?

"So you think I did it, is that what you're saying?" I said. "Thanks a lot!"

He studied me a moment, just like Levesque would have, only Steve's eyes are blue, not black, and they're warm even when he's trying to come across as stern and impenetrable.

"Tell you what," he said. "If you want to volunteer your fingerprints, I may be able to clear you."

"What do you mean? You found prints on the car?"

"On the car? Sure, but they're probably Green's. I found what looks like the implement that was used to smash the window."

That was news.

"Where did you find it?"

"I can't tell you that."

"What is it?"

"I can't tell you that, either, Chloe."

"How do you know it was used to break into the car?"

He gave me a sour look. "This is what I do for a living," he said.

He was offering me a break. He was going to get me off the hook.

"Okay," I said. "You can fingerprint me."

The process took a couple of minutes and left me with inky fingers. "So?" I said.

"So, you have to give me time to take a good look."

"How about if I come back at lunchtime?"

"Sure."

"And, Steve?"

"I know. Don't tell the chief."

"Thanks, Steve."

* * *

I saw Davis heading for the back entrance to the school.

"Hey!" I called.

He didn't even turn around. I broke into a run and caught up with him as he reached for the door handle.

"Hey, Davis!"

He glanced at me, then yanked the door open. I reached around him and shoved it shut.

"I'm talking to you," I said.

"Actually, you're yelling at me. I'd appreciate it if you'd lower the volume a little."

"I would have appreciated it if you'd turned up at the library yesterday like you were supposed to," I said.

"Something came up."

He reached for the door handle again. I grabbed him by the arm. He spun around to face me. He looked terrible. His face was grayish and his eyes were watery, as if he'd had too little sleep or too much partying. But if he expected any sympathy

117

from me, he was headed for disappointment.

"I don't like being stood up, Davis, and I don't like being taken advantage of."

"How exactly did I take advantage of you?"

"You're expecting me to do all the work."

"Says who? Look, not that it's any of your business, but my grandmother is sick. She was up all night last night. I hardly slept at all. But I read the book, and if you want, we can get together after school today. Okay?"

"You read the book?" I didn't want to believe him, but there was something in his voice and in the way he was looking at me that persuaded me that he was telling the truth. "The whole book, from start to finish?"

"Every page," he said.

"Okay. Meet me in the library after school."

"I'll be there."

* * *

I got caught out in French class. Madame Benoit asked me a question that I didn't hear because I was running the possibilities over and over in my mind. A crib sheet had been found under my desk, written in what looked like my handwriting. Someone had punctured one of Mr. Green's tires and left a calling card behind — a purple pen that just happened to be identical to the kind of pen I used. Someone had broken into Mr. Green's car and stolen a file and left behind another calling card that everyone associated with me. And, of course, Mr. Green blamed me. Under the circumstances, even I would have blamed me. The only trouble was that I was the only person who knew for sure that I had done none of the things I had been accused of. But if it wasn't me, then who was it? Who had a big enough grudge against me to want to get me in that kind of trouble? Daria? Rick? Davis? Sarah? It was a depressing number of possibilities. To get at the culprit, I'd have to eliminate them one by one. Meanwhile, Steve was clearing my name.

I dropped by the cafeteria at lunchtime. My plan was to grab a sandwich to eat on the way to the police station, where I was going to check in with Steve. I was standing in line when I spotted Sarah sitting at one end of a crowded table, reading while she nibbled a muffin and sipped juice out of a bottle with a straw. I stared at her for a few moments, watching her hand wrapped around the smooth glass of the bottle. When I got to the head of the line to pay, I asked Nicole Amberley, who worked the cash, if she had any plastic bags. She looked at me blankly.

"Maybe behind the counter somewhere," I suggested.

She poked around behind the cash and finally fished out a used plastic grocery bag. I thanked her, folded the bag and tucked it into my jeans pocket. Then I carried my sandwich over to the vacant seat opposite Sarah.

"Mind if I sit here?" I asked.

She started to say something as she pulled her

eyes away from her book, but when she saw who it was her mouth clamped shut.

"Hey, Sarah, how's it going?" I said.

She bent to her book again.

I reached out with my hand, trying to make the movement seem perfectly innocent. Then, oops, somehow I managed to knock over her juice bottle. Apple juice streamed across the table. Sarah leapt up to avoid getting soaked. She grabbed her books to get them out of the way.

"Geez, sorry," I said. I thought I sounded convincingly contrite. I caught the bottle at the rim and picked it up carefully.

"You did that on purpose," she shrieked at me.

"I said I was sorry."

But she wasn't listening. At first she was too busy shoving her books into her bag. Then she was too busy stomping out of the cafeteria. I sat where I was, munching my sandwich. After everyone had stopped staring at me, I fished the plastic bag out of my pocket. Then, careful to hold the bottle by the rim, I slipped it inside. I took it with me when I went to the police station.

Levesque wasn't there. Good. But neither was Steve. The door was open, though, so he had to be close by. I went over to his desk. His computer was on. Maybe that was a good sign and maybe it wasn't. Sitting beside it was a thick book. I turned it around to see what it was. Fingerprints. The whole book was about fingerprints — the latest techniques for lifting them and enhancing them. I smiled. Steve was a lot younger than Levesque. This was his first job and he'd only had it for two years. I usually thought of him as a rookie. But he took his job seriously and he was always learning. This book was proof of it.

A door opened behind me. I whirled around. It was Steve.

"So?" I said, trying to sound casual, as if I hadn't been snooping, "What did you find out?"

"Maybe I should be asking that question," he said, circling around his desk to check his computer screen. He seemed relieved by whatever was on it. "I found pretty much what I expected. Your fingerprints don't match the print I found on the bar — "

Aha. So the implement used to smash Mr. Green's window had been a bar of some kind.

"How do you know that the bar you found was used to smash the window?" I asked.

"Aw, come on, Chloe," he said.

"I won't tell anyone."

He glanced around, as if he half-expected Levesque to pop out from behind a closed door.

"Steve, I'm innocent, remember? I'm also curious. How did you tie the bar to the crime?"

"I found it under the hedge not far from the parking lot," he said. "It's a metal bar, painted black. The paint was scratched in a couple of places. I found flecks of black paint on a couple of the pieces of glass in the car."

"But those pieces of glass were tiny."

"Give me a little credit," he said. "I know how to use a microscope." When I looked surprised, he said, "This may be a small department, but we're all professionals here." I don't think it was my imagination that he stood a little taller when he said that.

I opened the plastic bag I was carrying and carefully pulled out the juice bottle.

"I'm pretty sure there's some good prints on this," I said. "And I think the person who belongs to them may have had something to do with that break-in."

He peered at the bottle. His lips twitched. I realized that he was fighting back laughter.

"What?" I said, indignant.

"I think you've been watching too much TV."

"Come on, Steve. Someone's been setting me up."

He looked at the bottle again. "You want me to check it for prints? See if anything I find matches the prints on the bar?"

I nodded.

He pondered this for a moment. "I don't see why not," he said at last. "I'm supposed to be looking into this. I guess this counts as looking."

I set the bottle onto his desk, thanked him, and headed back to school.

* * *

Davis was leaning against a bank of lockers in the corridor outside the school library after classes.

"You're late," he said.

"By two minutes," I said. "*You're* twenty-four hours late."

He pulled his backpack off, rooted around inside it, and produced a small sheaf of paper. He handed it to me.

"What's this?" I asked.

"It's an analysis of the social issues in *Spartacus*," he said. "Slavery. The human quest for freedom even at the cost of death. The effect that a rebellion, even a failed rebellion, can have on society. That kind of stuff."

I flipped through the papers. Nearly ten pages, typed.

"It's good for an A, trust me," he said. "You want to put your name on it, that's fine with me."

"I don't want to just put *my* name on *your* work. This is supposed to be a team project."

"Whatever," he said. "You can add to it." He glanced at his watch. "We done here?"

"Yeah," I said. "I guess."

After he left, I stayed in the library and read what he had given to me. It sounded pretty good. Maybe too good.

* * *

I stopped by the newspaper office after my meeting with Davis. One of the computers has Internet access. That was the one I was interested in. I waited patiently until Eric had finished checking out whatever he was checking out. Then I sat down, went to my favorite search engine, and typed in the words I had typed in only a couple of days before. It didn't take long to find what I was looking for.

I was on my way out of school when I spotted Daria. She was standing near the front entrance, glancing up and down the halls as if she were looking for someone. She straightened up when she saw me and started walking toward me. I glanced back over my shoulder to see if there was someone behind me. There wasn't. She came right up to me.

"Hi," she said. She seemed nervous, which made me instantly suspicious.

Maybe I should have made an effort to sound friendly. Maybe I would have if she hadn't spent the last few months acting as if I were invisible, when she didn't seem to be wishing that I'd be hit by a bus.

In response to her wavering "Hi," I said, "What?" You could say it came out sounding like a snarl.

One of Daria's feet shuffled backward. The other stayed firmly in place. She seemed to be trying to decide whether to stay or to go.

"You don't always have to act so superior," she said.

Superior? Me? Which one of us had been going around with her nose in the air for the past few months?

"Is that it? Is that all you want to say to me?" I said. Daria liked me even less than I had imagined if, after months of the silent treatment, her first words to me were words of criticism. In fact . . . "It's you, isn't it?" I said.

Both of her feet shuffled backward now.

"What's me?"

"Someone has been trying to make me look bad. It's you, isn't it?"

I couldn't have gotten a bigger reaction if I had slapped her.

"You think you're so smart," she said. Gone was her nervousness. Gone was her quiet little voice. "You think you're better than everyone else. Well, you're not smart and you sure aren't better."

With that she wheeled and flew down the hall. I almost called her back. I should have. I was sure that what she had ended up saying wasn't what she had started out to say. I should have listened before I spoke. I should have suggested that we sit down and talk. I should have offered to buy her a bottle of juice.

* * *

I stopped by the *Beacon* office on the off chance that Davis would be there. He wasn't. I headed for his house — and got lucky.

I saw him as soon as I turned off Centre Street. He was halfway up Macdonald Avenue at the end of his grandmother's driveway. He wasn't alone. There was a guy with him. As I got closer, I recognized him. He was the guy I'd seen with Davis that Saturday when I'd been working on my history essay. I didn't know his name, though. He was facing me. Davis was sort of sideways and didn't see me. The guy I didn't know handed something to Davis. It looked like an envelope of some kind. Davis opened it and pulled something out. He looked at whatever it was, then he said something. From the tension in his body and the way he jerked his arms, it looked like he was arguing with the guy. I was a couple of houses away when the guy poked Davis on the shoulder with a finger. He looked angry. He poked Davis a couple more times, then turned and headed up the street in the opposite direction from me. Good old Davis — making friends all over town.

I reached the end of the driveway just as Davis disappeared into the garage. Nice try. He was going to have to leave the country if he wanted to avoid me. I ran up the driveway and pushed open the small door Davis had gone through. I found him inside, crouched on the concrete floor in front of the car. It took me a moment to realize that he was burning something.

"Here," I said, taking a sheaf of paper out of my pocket. It was the essay Davis had given me at school. "Add this to your fire."

Davis whirled around. The look of stunned surprise on his face brought a smile to mine.

"You may want to think about controlling the flames," I suggested. Little bits of whatever he was destroying were floating up into the air. He stared down at the small blaze, but did nothing to contain it. I caught a glimpse of part of a paper that hadn't completely burned. It looked like a photograph.

"What are you doing here?" he demanded.

"I thought I'd tell you before I tell Ms. Peters," I said.

"Tell her what? What are you talking about?"

"You're a cheat, Davis."

He smiled at me and shook his head. "I think you've got that backwards," he said. "You're the cheat. You got nailed for it, remember?"

"And now *you're* going to get nailed. How stupid do you think Ms. Peters is?"

"I don't know what you mean."

"Right. Next you're going to tell me that this so-called essay is your own work."

I had to hand it to him, he kept right on smiling as if nothing were wrong.

"This may look like a hick town to you, Davis. But we know all about the Internet up here. We're as wired as anyone else. I know how to do research on the Net. And I have a pretty good memory for what I turn up."

Still no reaction.

"You got this off the Internet," I said. "I know exactly where you found it and I can show Ms. Peters."

"Show her what?" he said. "That I did some research on the Net? So what?"

"That you tried to pass off the work as your own."

"Did I?"

He was so cool.

"Davis, you gave me this and said it was your work."

Up went one golden eyebrow. "I don't remember saying it was my work. I said it was an analysis of *Spartacus*, and it is."

"You said I could put my name on it if I wanted to."

"I thought that's the way you operated, you know, what with the way you act in Mr. Green's class," he said. "My mistake, I guess."

I don't believe in violence. Okay, so I had shoved him once. I felt bad about that, and not just because I was afraid of getting into trouble for it. I felt bad because violence doesn't solve anything. But at that exact moment I was wishing I were the kind of person who could make a rock-hard fist and deliver a knockout blow. Davis just never let up.

"I don't want to work with you anymore," I said. I probably sounded like a little kid. *I don't want to play with you anymore.*

He shrugged. "I didn't exactly beg Ms. Peters to let me work with you. If you have a problem with us as a team, do something about it."

"I'm going to write my own essay and hand it in," I said. "You can either do one yourself or not. I don't care."

He stared at me for a moment. He didn't show any emotion. He didn't seem to care one way or another.

"We done here?" he said.

"Here, there and everywhere."

On the way down the driveway, I ran into Sarah. She couldn't have looked more surprised if Dracula himself had stepped out of Davis's garage. She watched me walk down the drive. Then she went looking for Davis.

"You sure you don't want to come?" Levesque said at supper.

"I'm sure," I said.

"Phoebe's coming," he said. "I'm picking her up after school. We'll be in Toronto by early evening. Your mother's train gets in at ten. We're staying overnight. I have a couple of appointments on Saturday — "

"Oh," I said. "So it's a business trip?"

"Partly," he admitted. "There are a few things that I need to look into."

"Stanley Meadows things?"

He nodded. "Why don't you come? You might have a good time."

I shook my head. I now had a team project for English that I was doing alone. Ms. Peters was going to be less than thrilled about the situation, especially after she had made it clear to me that I had to get along with Davis. To come out of this with a halfway decent grade, I was going to have to produce a superlatively superlative essay.

"I have too much work to do," I said. "Don't worry. I'll be fine." When he continued to look unhappy, I added, "I'll check in with Ross. I'll check in with his mother, too, if you want." When he still didn't seem satisfied, I said, "I'm not a little kid." Then, finally, "I'll call Steve and give him a status report, too, and he can call you. But I can't afford to go to Toronto this weekend. No way."

My mention of Steve seemed to do it. He nodded.

"Just one thing, though," he said.

Groan. There was a condition coming, I could feel it.

"I'm chief of police around here," he said.

"Yeah. So?"

"So I'm the person who decides what forensic work gets done," he said.

I gave him my best I-don't-know-what-you're-talking-about look. As usual, it didn't work.

"You hear me, Chloe?" he said.

"You found out about the fingerprints, huh?"

"That does not happen again," he said. "Ever. Understand?"

"But someone is trying to frame me — "

"It doesn't happen again, right, Chloe?"

Sigh. "It doesn't happen again." But I couldn't stop myself from asking, "So, did he find out anything?"

"About?"

He was wearing his cop expression, the one that made it impossible to tell what he was thinking and, I admit, it rattled me. Maybe all he knew was that I had volunteered my fingerprints to Steve. Maybe he didn't know that I had also volunteered Sarah's. Should I press the point or not?

"Never mind," I said.

"When Steve looks in on you, you're not to bother him," Levesque said.

Double groan. "Now *Steve's* going to look in on me?"

I couldn't prove it, but I was pretty sure that

somewhere under his bushy moustache, Levesque was smiling. Okay, fine. If that's what he wanted, that's what he'd get. Nothing I could do was going to change it. No biggie.

"I mean it, Chloe. You're not to waste his time with any more irrelevant fingerprints, or anything else, for that matter."

"I heard you."

"Did you?"

Then it clicked. *Irrelevant* fingerprints. Sarah's fingerprints. They didn't match the ones Steve had found on the bar.

Strike one.

Chapter 11

The next day, what started out as a regular morning quickly turned into a nightmare morning.

The regular part of the morning: I got up, got dressed, drank a big, strong cup of coffee while toasting a bagel, gathered my school stuff, strapped on my backpack and hiked to school, stopping on the way to call on Ross. We chitchatted while walking — I got brought up to date on the number of responses to the reader survey. I was surprised that people cared enough to fill out the survey and drop it in the box inside the newspaper office. I got to school in plenty of time to dump my backpack on the floor in front of my locker and arrange my books. I noticed there were posters for tonight's school dance everywhere. I also noticed, but didn't pay attention to, Sarah Moran, who turned to look at me like I was a cockroach or a rat or some other vermin. Maybe Davis hadn't told her why I had been in his garage. Maybe she thought I was trying to steal him. Right. I ignored her.

I started to organize books for my morning class-

es. Then there was a commotion down the hall —
two guys were shoving each other. I took a few
steps in their direction to see what was going on. I
couldn't help it. School wasn't the most exciting
place in the world, so when two Neanderthals
started in on each other, it was just natural that I
wanted to catch a glimpse. Besides, it was always
fun to see Mr. Moore, one of the vice-principals,
charging down the hall, face flushed, jaw clenched,
ready to break things up. He acted like a TV cop —
"All right, people, move it along, there's nothing to
see here" — and handed out detention slips to the
two guys. I turned back to my locker. A little way
down the hall, Daria was standing close to Rick.
She was saying something to him and she didn't
look happy. Rick looked annoyed. Trouble in
Loveland? A person can hope, right? Then the
homeroom bell rang and, hello, it was terminal
boredom time, *again*.

A regular good morning turns into a nightmare
morning: This played out like a train wreck in slow
motion. It began — where else? — in Mr. Green's
classroom.

There's always a minute or two at the beginning
of each class when people are filing in, finding
their seats, talking to each other. This can be
shorter or longer, depending on whether the
teacher is already in the classroom. In this case,
he wasn't. Rick was sitting on Daria's desk, talking to her. He wasn't smiling the way he usually
did. And he seemed to be doing all the talking,

only it came out like a low whine. I didn't know what he was talking about and I told myself that I didn't care. But I did care, because it sounded like the relationship was in trouble. I knew it wasn't nice, but if Rick and trouble appeared in the same sentence and the trouble applied to Rick, hey, you have to treasure life's simple pleasures, right?

Wherever Rick was, Brad was. This morning he was standing on the other side of Daria's desk. Daria didn't look at me. Sarah was standing next to my desk, talking to Davis. Davis was slumped in his chair, dressed in black, as usual, and wearing his sunglasses, even though he had been told maybe a million times that it wasn't allowed in school. Sarah sounded upset about something. I heard her say the word "dance." There was a dance at the school that night. It sounded like she wanted him to go. It sounded like he wasn't making any commitment.

I dumped my books on top of my desk and sat down. Mr. Green came into the room. Everyone headed for their places. Mr. Green threaded his way up and down the rows of desks, collecting essays that were due. Someone behind me made a rude noise. I turned to look, along with almost everyone else. That's when it happened. I don't know who did it because I wasn't looking. It could have been Rick or Brad or Sarah. It could even have been Daria. She could have done it with her elbow. Or maybe it wasn't anyone's fault. Maybe I had set my books too close to the edge of my desk.

Whoever or whatever was responsible, the result was this: Two textbooks and two binders, both mine, crashed to the floor just as Mr. Green started down my row. Loose papers slid in all directions on the floor. While I jumped up to collect them, Mr. Green looked down at my stuff, which was spread out at his feet. I don't know for sure — it's one of those things you can never know for sure — but it seemed to me that at the exact same time that I was thinking *hey, where did* that *come from?* he was thinking *aha!*

We both bent down at the same time. If I hadn't stopped halfway and straightened up again, we would have played like a scene from a bad sitcom. You know, two characters bend over to pick up the same thing and end up knocking their heads together. Even though we didn't physically crash, still the eastbound train that was Mr. Green was fated to slam into the westbound train that was me. My life was about to go hurtling off the rails and there was absolutely nothing I could do to stop it.

Mr. Green straightened up slowly. He stared at the neatly typed and stapled sheaf of paper he now clutched in one hand. Then he raised his eyes to look at me.

The words sprang to my lips: *I didn't do anything.* I choked them back. He would never believe me. I glanced around the classroom to see if anyone understood what had just happened. Some people weren't paying any attention to what was going on.

Those who were watching were divided into two groups. One group seemed to know that something had just happened, but wasn't sure what it was. Another, smaller group of people who were close enough to see the papers on the floor before Mr. Green picked them up, knew exactly what had just happened and were wondering what was going to happen next. Daria kept facing straight ahead. Rick grinned at me. So did Brad. Davis hadn't moved. He was slumped in his seat, sunglasses shielding his eyes. Sarah stared at me.

Sarah.

Sarah, whose locker was directly opposite mine.

Sarah, who didn't like me.

Sarah, who had been standing at her locker, shooting daggers at me only that morning.

Sarah, who had had the opportunity, while my back was turned and I was watching the fight in the hall, to stuff that paper into one of my binders.

Sarah, who had a supply of purple pens she never used. Okay, so her fingerprints weren't on the bar Steve Denby had found. Who said the prints he had found belonged to the person who had broken into Mr. Green's car? Maybe Sarah was as smart at car-breaking as she was at school. Maybe she had worn gloves.

I scooped my things off the floor and headed for the door.

"Where do you think you're going?" Mr. Green yelled after me.

Where did he think I was going?

I headed for the office. He had caught up to me by the time I got there.

"I don't understand you," he said. We were standing in the hall outside of the administration office. "Why are you doing this to me?"

I looked at him. His face was covered in red splotches. His eyes were watery. If he had been anyone except Mr. Green, I would have thought he was close to tears. I considered answering his question, but what could I say that I hadn't said a dozen times already? I went into the office and sat on the bench. He followed and talked to Ms. Jeffries. I don't know what he said. They disappeared into her private office. They were in there for what felt like ages. When Mr. Green finally emerged, he didn't look at me. I was waiting for Ms. Jeffries to summon me into her office and expel me for good when something strange happened.

Daria came into the office. She went up to the counter and, in a low, calm voice, asked one of the secretaries if she could please speak to Ms. Jeffries.

"It's important," she said.

While the secretary picked up the phone and called into Ms. Jeffries's office, Daria turned to me. She didn't say anything. The secretary told her she could go in. Daria rounded the edge of the counter and headed down the corridor to the principal's office. The door closed behind her. When she came out nearly ten minutes later, Ms. Jeffries was with her.

"I think you can go back to class now, Chloe," she said.

"But what — "

"You can go, too, Daria. I'll talk to you later."

"Yeah, but — " I said.

Too late. Ms. Jeffries was already on her way back to her office. As she passed by the secretary she said, "Ask Mr. Green to come and see me when he has a moment."

Daria got to the door first. She held it open for me.

"I told her I did it," she said, as we walked side by side down the hall.

Whoa! I stopped and stared at her. Classes had changed. The hall was deserted.

"Are you telling me that *you* broke into Mr. Green's car?"

She gave me a withering look. "Of course not. I'm not that stupid," she said. "I told her I found Mr. Green's paper in the garbage and that I put it in your binder."

"Why would you do that?"

"As a joke. Because everyone thinks you have it in for Mr. Green. So when I found the paper, I planted it in your things. I thought it would be funny." She flashed me a contrite look. "It showed very poor judgment on my part," she said, speaking the words as if she were reciting lines from a play.

It was an interesting story, but it didn't sound right. If she had planted the stolen paper in my binder to make me look guilty of breaking into Mr. Green's car, why would she suddenly decide to march down to the office and confess to the crime, even if she had done it in a way that minimized her guilt? Why confess at all? No one suspected her, except maybe me. For sure no one had any proof that she had done anything wrong. I wasn't sure about all the details, but there was one thing I would have been willing to stake my life on.

"You didn't actually have anything to do with it, did you, Daria?"

"Hey, you, girls!" Mr. Moore strode vice-principally toward us. "Why aren't you in class?"

"We just came from the office," Daria said.

"Get to class," he said. "Now."

Daria sped toward the stairs to go to her next class. My class was in the opposite direction. It was going to drive me crazy, but I would have to wait to get any answers out of her.

* * *

All Mr. Moore had done was send Daria to her next class, but the effect was the same as if he'd banished her to Pluto. I scanned the hallways as I moved through the rest of the morning, but I didn't see her anywhere. I spent my entire lunch hour looking for her, first in the cafeteria, then in the halls, then in the schoolyard, and finally around town. I was almost late to my first class of the afternoon. I looked for her after school too. At least, I started to. I was at my locker, stashing my books, when Phoebe called my name.

"Dad wants to talk to you," she shouted down the hall. "He's outside in the car."

There were a few other people in the hall. None

of them even looked in my direction, but I still didn't appreciate Phoebe shouting like that. It made me sound like a little kid. *Daddy wants to talk to you.* I followed her out to the parking lot, where Levesque was sitting in the car.

"Here's the phone number of the hotel," he said, handing me a folded piece of paper. "And you have my cell phone number, right?"

Of course I had his cell phone number. And he could have left the other number for me on the family bulletin board — the fridge. There was something else coming.

"Don't get into any more trouble," he said, "no matter how tempting it gets."

He made more trouble sound like a box of chocolates, absolutely irresistible. In actual fact, more trouble was like a year's worth of Friday afternoon detentions, something I wanted to avoid at all costs.

"I'm going down to the newspaper office," I told him. "Then I'm going home and I'm going to spend the weekend doing homework."

"You're not going to the dance?" Phoebe asked. If you were to draw a picture of her voice, you'd have to draw bulging eyes and a mouth shaped like a big O. Phoebe wouldn't have missed a school dance for anything. Well, almost anything. She had been planning to go to this one with a bunch of her friends, but had changed her plans when she had the chance to drive down to Toronto.

I, on the other hand, hadn't been planning to go,

and still wasn't. I hate school dances. First of all, I don't like to dance. Second, if I ever had the urge to dance with someone, I sure wouldn't want to do it with a team of high school teachers watching me. Finally, every school dance I had ever gone to had featured three things: a group of guys who tried to smuggle in booze; at least one pathetic girl crying in the bathroom because her boyfriend or recently ex-boyfriend or the guy she wished was her boyfriend was making eyes at someone else; and one or more teachers knocking themselves out trying to be cool, which is pretty much mission impossible. All of these were things I could live happily ever after without.

"No, I'm not going to the dance," I told Phoebe. "Maybe I'll rent some movies."

At least, that was my original plan.

Chapter 12

I watched Levesque's car pull out of the parking lot and head up toward Centre Street. I was on my own. For the first time in longer than I could remember, I had the house to myself. Not just for a couple of hours, but for a couple of days. They wouldn't be back until Sunday. It was enough to make me wish I had a million friends and loved to party. Oh, well.

I headed back into the school to look for Ross. Now that I actually had a weekend to myself, with no one looking over my shoulder or asking me where I was going and when I was planning to be back, it would be a shame not to have at least some fun. Maybe Ross would want to do something.

"Like what?" he said.

"I don't know. How about a movie?"

There were two movies playing at the local cinema. Ross had seen one of them. The other was the latest animated feature from Disney.

"No way I'm going to that," he said.

Like I had been planning to pressure him into it.

"We could go hiking," he said. He liked outdoor activities.

"Yeah, okay." I was getting to like them too. "How about tomorrow?"

"Tomorrow's great. Meet you at noon at the park entrance."

I was almost at the door to the office when Ross said, "You going to the dance tonight?"

The word that popped into my mind was, no. The word that actually came out of my mouth was, "Why?"

He shrugged. "Just wondering."

"Who would I go with?" I asked. "Rick Antonio?"

"I thought maybe I'd go," he said.

Ross dancing? I tried to picture it. He's a nice guy. Actually, he's a very nice guy. But imagining Ross on the dance floor made me think of a loaf of Wonder bread shimmying around, trying to look hip.

"Who are you going with?" I asked. He hadn't shown any interest in anyone since Tessa Nixon.

He shrugged. "No one," he said. "I just thought it might be fun."

"Right," I said with a snort. "What could be more fun than observing the three basic food groups at a high school dance?"

"Three basic food groups?"

"The people who are kissing each other, the people who are dreaming about kissing that someone special, and the people who are whining and crying because someone else is kissing their someone special. No, thanks! Have a ball, Ross."

* * *

To get from the newspaper office to the exit, I had to pass the gym. One of the doors stood partially open. As I went past it I noticed a bunch of people inside, decorating the place in preparation for tonight. I stopped and wondered if Daria was there. She struck me as the gym-decorating type. Then it hit me. She had probably earned a detention for her confession. I checked my watch. If she was sitting out a detention, she'd be there for another couple of minutes. I headed for the second-floor classroom that served as the detention hall.

It was deserted.

I heard something behind me. The door to the girls' bathroom at the end of the hall was just kicking shut. Daria? I hurried toward it. Sure enough, someone was inside. Inside and crying. Geez, what is it with girls' bathrooms? I bet you never found guys crying their eyes out in the boys' room.

As soon as she heard the door open, Sarah turned her back to it and cranked on the cold water faucet. Then she ducked and splashed water on her face. I think the idea was to camouflage her tears. The tap water didn't do much for her puffy eyes, though.

Okay, so now I had two choices. One, turn around and walk away, leaving her to her private tear-fest. If she had wanted company, she would have picked a more public place to let loose, right? Or, two, be all concerned and sympathetic and ask her what the matter was. Like we were friends. Like I cared.

I hate decisions like that. I hate when you know what you *should* do, which is the admirable, noble thing, but what you should do is pretty much the last thing on earth you actually *want* to do. I sighed.

"You okay, Sarah?"

"Go away."

Her response gave me license to leave with a clear conscience, right? I had tried to be nice and she had rejected me.

The key word, of course, was conscience. My problem is that I actually have one. And Sarah's eyes were as puffy as a couple of Mom's popovers. Water — tears or tap water or a combination of both — was trickling down her cheeks and dripping from her chin.

"You want to talk about it?" I asked.

Her puffy eyes narrowed. Their redness turned to fire.

"*My* life is none of *your* business," she said. She tried to coax some paper towel out of the dispenser on the wall near the sink, but it was either jammed or empty. She blotted at her face with the palms of her hands. "I have to get back to the gym."

Okay, fine. Now she had definitely given me an out. My help wasn't wanted. There was nothing more for me to do. Except:

"I don't know what your problem is," I said. I was letting loose with my anger, not what you'd call a sensitive move. But she'd been unfair to me. She kept on being unfair to me no matter what I did, no matter how nice I tried to be. "What did I ever do to you?"

She started to cry again. Actually, she blubbered. It was not a pretty sight.

"Okay, okay, I'm *sorry,*" I said.

"No," she said. *"I'm* sorry. I should have done something."

Huh?

She disappeared into one of the cubicles and I heard the *thwick-thwick* of a couple of pieces of industrial-strength toilet tissue being yanked from a little metal dispenser. She came out again, drying her eyes. She might have had a shot at succeeding, too, if she hadn't been crying at the same time.

"It's D-Davis," she said.

"Davis is a jerk," I told her. "Don't waste your time crying over him."

Her lower lip started to tremble.

"He is a jerk sometimes," she said, sounding fierce. She snuffled. When she spoke again her voice was as soft as a week-old kitten. "I'm worried about him."

"You really like him, don't you?"

She nodded. There was just no accounting for some people's taste in other people.

"You said you were sorry, Sarah. What about?"

She blotted her eyes with the soggy toilet tissue. "I'm the one who forged your handwriting on those crib notes," she said. The words tumbled from her mouth, as if she were shoving them out and was relieved to be rid of them. Maybe Levesque was right. Maybe most wrongdoers really do want to unburden themselves.

I felt like a cartoon character who had just been hammered with a wooden mallet. The world tilted. I seemed to be standing at a crazy angle. I practically saw stars circling my head.

"You?" I said. "Why?"

"D-Davis," she said. "He asked me to."

"Do you do everything Davis asks you to?" I said. Now I was yelling. Now I was angry.

Her head hung even lower. "He says you always act like you know everything. He says you're one of those people who thinks she's smarter than everyone else."

Talk about the pot calling the kettle black, as my mom would have said!

"You've been giving him a hard time ever since he got here," she said. "It's not his fault his father is rich. It's not his fault he went to a private school."

"Yeah, but it's his fault he never lets anyone forget it. He sounds just like — " I stopped abruptly.

Sarah frowned at me. "Just like what?"

The thought had just popped into my mind, but now that it was there, I knew it was true. "He sounds just like me when I first moved here," I said. Well, except for the rich thing. And the private school thing. And the Toronto thing. I never realized how obnoxious I must have been.

"You never let up," Sarah said. "He's not that

bad. And he really is smart. Did you ever read his articles on street kids?"

I admitted that I hadn't.

"Or see his video? He's working on a screenplay that's amazing. There's this guy in it. He's a thief — "

I hated to interrupt her, but, "Sarah, about the crib notes. You actually forged my handwriting because Davis wanted you to?" I know people do crazy things when they're in love, but *this?*

"He said you needed to be taught a lesson." Her chin drooped again. "I agreed with him. You — " She looked at me.

"What?"

"I just thought . . . well, you're always cutting people up. He said he wondered what people would think of the great Chloe Yan if it turned out she had cheated her way onto the honor roll. He wondered how many loyal friends you had. He said he bet it wouldn't be many."

Cheated my way onto the honor roll?

"So you forged my writing — " I still couldn't believe it.

"And Davis sort of slid it under your desk when you weren't looking."

"*Sort of* slid it."

"And he was right," she said. "When people saw it, they believed it. Everyone thought you were cheating."

I couldn't believe this was happening to me. "You guys set me up? Because I teased Davis?"

"I said I was sorry." She sounded defensive now.

But not nearly as defensive as I would have liked. "I was mad at you," she added. More tears welled up in her eyes. "I'm so ashamed of myself."

"Geez, what did I ever do to you?"

"I've always been at the top of the class," she whispered, her voice shaky.

"Well, excuse me for working hard and getting good grades."

She dabbed at some more tears.

"I guess after you landed me in trouble the first time, you just couldn't stop yourself, is that it, Sarah?" I said. "What were you aiming for, to get me expelled? Were you trying to remove the competition once and for all?"

She said nothing.

"The flat tire and the car break-in," I said. "That was you, too, wasn't it?"

"No," she said quickly. She shook her head as if she were trying to shake a hat off it. "I didn't have anything to do with any of that."

"But Davis did."

"I — I don't know."

"Sarah, you just said it was his idea to forge my handwriting."

"If he did the other things, he never told me. I had nothing to do with them, honest." She hesitated. "Maybe he did it," she said. "I don't know. He's been acting so strange lately. He says it's all the work he's been doing on his screenplay."

The famous screenplay.

"He's applying for the summer program at the

Canadian Film Institute. He has to send his script to them before exams. And he's been hanging around with this guy who gives me the creeps. He says the guy is helping him with research."

Oh? I flashed back to the guy I had seen at Davis's house yesterday. I'd seen Davis with him before, too.

"Who is he?" I asked.

Sarah hesitated. At first I thought she wasn't going to answer. Then she shook her head.

"His name is Gary, that's all I know."

"You mean, you don't actually know him? Isn't he from around here?" I had assumed that he was, but if Sarah didn't know him, then maybe I was wrong.

She shook her head. "I don't know. All I know is that Davis has been hanging out with him. And whenever he does, he gets all worked up, you know, all excited, but he won't tell me what it's all about. And then lately . . . " Her voice trailed off. "I'm worried about him."

"Is that why you're in here crying?"

I probably shouldn't have mentioned crying. It got the waterworks flowing again.

"That," she said, dabbing at her eyes again with her wad of damp toilet tissue, "and feeling guilty about what I did to you and feeling ashamed of myself." She hesitated again. "If Davis did that stuff," she said finally, "if he punctured Mr. Green's tire and broke into his car — " She shook her head. "Davis is supposed to come to the dance with me tonight."

Yeah? "So?"

"Mr. Green is going to be here. He's one of the chaperones."

I thought about this. "You don't think Davis would try something else, do you?" I asked. But a good part of me thought he would. He seemed like the kind of guy who, now that he had taken a dislike to me, wasn't going to quit until he had me good and nailed.

"I don't know," Sarah said. "What should I do?"

"Are you really sorry for what you did to me?"

She nodded.

"You want to make it up to me?"

This time she nodded like a three-year-old who'd just been offered a double scoop of ice cream if she promised to be good.

"Don't tell Davis you talked to me, okay?"

Her nod was more tentative this time. But her voice was firm and determined. "Okay."

If she kept her word, maybe I'd have a chance.

As I pushed open the door, something else ate at me. Davis's little frame-up had worked. He had guessed right. He had set me up, and instead of believing in me, people had believed the lies. Okay, so you could argue that that said something about them. But the thing I couldn't shake, the thing that stuck in my throat and made it hard for me to breathe, was that it also said something about me. And what it said, I didn't like.

* * *

I packed my mini-knapsack carefully and slung it

over my best red sweater. I leaned into the mirror and brushed on some mascara. Then I stood well back to check how I looked. The sweater fit me perfectly and looked terrific with my black skirt. On my way downstairs I passed by Phoebe's room. I peeked in. Her cell phone was sitting on her desk. She hadn't taken it to Toronto. I put out of my mind all the times I had yelled at her for taking things of mine without asking permission. I grabbed her phone and tucked it into my knapsack along with the camera I had packed. You never know, I thought.

When I reached the front door, Shendor bounded over to me.

"No, girl," I told her. "You can't come."

She made pathetic puppy eyes at me.

"You've already had your walk," I told her, not that it did any good. Why do otherwise sane people talk to dogs as if dogs will understand and respond rationally? Dogs just aren't that bright. At least, my dog isn't. All she heard was the "walk" word. She rowfed optimistically.

When I got to school, I couldn't decide what to do — go inside or skulk around outside? I had arrived early on purpose, so I could see who was going in and out. But after a few minutes of hanging around in a dark corner of the parking lot, two things occurred to me. One, when I found Sarah in the bathroom, she had said she had to get back to the gym. I hadn't paid much attention to that at the time. But now I chewed it over.

Kids had been decorating the gym in the afternoon. If Sarah had to get back to the gym, then that meant she had been part of the decorating crew. And if that was true, then she was also on the dance organizing committee. And the dance organizing committee always showed up early to handle the ton of details that go into organizing a dance. If Sarah had showed up early, and if Davis was going to the dance with her, then there was a pretty good chance that Davis was already inside.

The second thing that occurred to me was that I looked suspicious. I was standing well away from the lights, so I couldn't be seen. That meant that I was also standing right beside the parking lot. Mr. Green was a chaperone. Mr. Green's car was in the parking lot somewhere. All I needed was for Mr. Green to see me out there and I'd be in trouble all over again.

I headed inside.

"Hey, Chloe!"

It was Ross. He was standing up near the deejay table when he spotted me. As he came toward me, he had a funny look on his face. He seemed to be hunting for something over my shoulder.

"I thought you weren't coming," he said.

"Change of plans."

He glanced over my shoulder again. "You here alone?"

"Are you seeing double or something, Ross? Do you see anyone with me?"

He laughed louder than the comment merited, and then seemed to relax.

"I thought you didn't like school dances."

"I don't," I said. "I'm not here for the dance."

"Oh? What *are* you here for?"

"I can't tell you that, Ross."

His look was a fairly good imitation of Shendor's please-please-*please*-take-me-for-a-walk expression.

"Okay, look, if I tell you, you have to keep your mouth shut and stay out of my way, okay?"

"They say the human body is ninety percent water," Ross said. "But they must be wrong because you're one hundred percent charm." I don't know what had been on his mind when I first came into the gym, but whatever it was, it had passed. He was back to his old self again.

I glanced around. Mr. Green was at the far end of the gym, talking with Ms. Pileggi, my math teacher and, I assumed, another of the chaperones. I nodded toward them.

"Your favorite teacher," Ross said. "What are you planning to do to him next?"

"Ha, ha," I said. "I thought you wanted to know why I'm here. I guess I must have misunderstood."

"Aw, come on, Chloe, can't you take a joke?"

"Sure. Tell me one." Then I decided to cut him some slack. "I think I know who's been messing with Mr. Green's car," I said. "And I want to try to catch that person in the act."

"Who is it?"

"I want to do this myself, Ross."

"Which means?"

"Which means you have to stay out of my way tonight. You can't pester me with a million questions. You can't follow me around. You can't nose into any conversations I have."

He shook his head. "One hundred percent pure charm," he muttered.

Davis didn't arrive until an hour after the dance had started. He was dressed completely in black, as usual, and had his sunglasses on when he came into the gym. Maybe that's why he hovered near the door and waited for Sarah to notice him — he couldn't see in the dim lighting. Sarah went over to him and draped her arms around his neck. He slipped a hand around her back. But their snuggling didn't last for long. Suddenly she pulled away from him. She was talking and shaking her head at the same time. I was too far away to hear what she was saying. Then she took him by the hand and dragged him to a corner of the gym farthest from the door. I was trying to keep an eye on them when someone slapped me on the back. I whirled around.

Rick.

He grinned at me.

"All alone, I see," he said. "And you with such a great personality. Go figure."

"Drop dead, Rick."

His grin widened. "See what I mean?"

I remembered the last time I had seen him and

Daria together — they had been arguing over something.

"Well, correct me if I'm wrong," I said, "but you seem to be flying solo tonight, too. Forget to take your popularity pills?"

I glanced around the gym to make my point about Daria being MIA but, to my surprise, I spotted her near the door. She had just come in and was scanning the room. She zeroed in on Rick and me and started walking toward us. Or, more likely, toward Rick.

Rick saw her, too, and his face brightened. He looked even more surprised than I was. I had probably been right, I decided. He had probably come to the dance alone.

"Hey, Daria," he said. He tried to slip his arm around her, but she wriggled away.

Yup, I had definitely been right.

"Aw, come on," he wheedled.

Daria ignored him. "Chloe, can I talk to you for a minute?" she said.

I glanced over to where Sarah and Davis had been standing and saw that Sarah was now alone. She looked miserable as she watched Davis disappear through an exit. Much as I wanted to find out why Daria had done what she had in the office that morning, I couldn't stay.

"I gotta go, Daria," I said. "Later, okay?"

"Let go of me, Rick," Daria said, slapping his hand away. She looked genuinely sorry to see me leave.

I spotted Davis in the darkness out behind the school. I figured he'd circle around to the parking lot, to Mr. Green's car. I figured wrong.

Chapter 13

Davis circled the school, but instead of heading for the parking lot, he took off in the opposite direction. He had a backpack slung from one shoulder. What was he up to? My first thought was, as long as it doesn't involve Mr. Green's car, I don't care. Then I wondered what other Mr. Green-related harm he might be cooking up. Sarah had said he'd been acting strangely. She was worried about him. Mostly she was worried about the things he was doing, which just happened to be things that ended up causing grief to me and my reputation. I decided to follow him. If he did anything else that was calculated to hurt me, I was ready for him.

Davis trotted across the schoolyard and out onto the street. From there, he headed north. At first I thought he was going home, but he steered clear of his own street and kept traveling due north until he reached Lodge Lake Road. He crossed the road and disappeared into the woods on the other side. I hesitated and almost turned back. Even after all these months, I had this thing about stumbling around in dark woods that might or might not contain wild creatures of various shapes and sizes, some of which have sharp teeth and big appetites. Call me chicken, but I don't want to end up on some bear's dinner menu. When I saw ribbons of light dancing through the woods ahead, first this way, then that, I realized that Davis was better equipped than I was. He had brought a flashlight with him. The only flash I had was the one built into the camera I had tucked into my mini-knapsack in the hope of catching Davis in the act. In the act of what, I wasn't sure. Where was he going, anyway? What was he up to? Did it have anything to do with why Sarah was so worried about him? I decided to follow him.

The ribbons of light got thinner and more distant. Davis was moving much faster than me. And why not? His way was well lit. He didn't have to worry about snagging his toe on some impossible-to-see loop of tree root sticking out of the ground. He was getting farther and farther ahead. If I didn't pick up my pace, I'd lose him. The good news was that Davis seemed to be keeping to a path. If I peered down and concentrated hard enough, I could just make out its outlines. I could even see the darker patches that were rocks and tree trunks. The only time I tripped was when I glanced ahead to get a fix on Davis. I stumbled over a rock and started hurtling forward. My mouth opened, but I stopped myself from calling out. I managed to regain my balance. No harm done.

The woods we were in weren't deep. They ended at 42 Sideroad. This section of it ran along the south and west sides of the park, and also along Little Lodge Lake, which was located mostly inside the park. When I reached the edge of the woods, I looked up and down the road. At first I saw no one. I crept out onto the strip of weedy grass that separated the woods from the road and took another look. To the west, I saw something moving. A person, loping along one shoulder of the road. He didn't have his flashlight on anymore, but I was sure it was Davis. I followed, keeping back as far as I could without losing him.

He was moving faster now, a guy in a big hurry. But in a hurry for what? Where was he going? It seemed pretty obvious that whatever he was up to, it had nothing to do with Mr. Green. But by now, I was hooked. I had never tailed anyone before. It's a weird kind of feeling. You get an inside look at someone's life, at what they do when they think no one is watching. It's kind of creepy and kind of fascinating all at the same time. Here was Davis Kaye, *très* cool, a guy who worked hard at projecting an image with his all-black wardrobe, his sunglasses that probably cost more than every piece of clothing I was wearing combined, his award-winning articles and award-winning video, and his I'm-writing-a-screenplay. Davis who didn't know that I knew what he had done to me. And here he was out in the night, headed somewhere, up to something — or maybe up to nothing at all — but clearly thinking that he was alone. Only he wasn't. Which made him wrong and me feel smart. Clever. *I know something you don't know, Davis. I know where you are and I see what you're doing.*

I followed him as the road wound between Little Lodge Lake and Elder Pond. Then, suddenly, the narrow ribbon of light danced up ahead again. I crept off the road and into the scrub. Davis wasn't moving now. The beam of his flashlight was aimed down. What was he doing? Then I realized — he was looking at something. A map, maybe? The light went off again, and Davis turned away from the road.

I waited until he was out of sight, then hurried to where he had been standing. A narrow gravel driveway cut off the side road and ran up toward Little Lodge Lake. He must have gone up there. I followed him. I stayed off the gravel — it was too noisy — and instead crept through the grass and weeds at the side of the driveway. Up ahead, I heard the muffled crunch of Davis's shoes on the gravel.

A small cottage slumped at the end of a twisting, pot-holed driveway. Did I say cottage? It looked more like a shack. Some of the places around the lake are huge. They're country mansions owned by city people who have lots of money and want all the comforts of home while they're supposedly roughing it in the woods. Then there are places that were built way back when, in the thirties or forties or fifties. They're small and basic, nothing more than places to sleep when you aren't swimming or canoeing or hiking in the park. Some of them leaned so far in one direction or the other that they seemed in danger of toppling over. The cottage at the end of the driveway was one of those.

I didn't see Davis, though. Where was he? And what was he doing here?

Something creaked in the darkness. I froze and glanced around, looking for cover. I couldn't figure out where the sound was coming from. And where was Davis? The cottage was completely dark, so he couldn't be inside. But if he wasn't there, where was he?

I peered around. Nothing. Then, off to my left, a narrow ribbon of light arced through the night and quickly vanished. Davis must be somewhere around the back of the cottage. My curiosity went into overdrive. Why was he here? What was he up to?

The cottage squatted in the middle of a weedy lawn that was ringed with scrub and trees. I scooted across the grass and crept around to the back, keeping myself hidden inside the perimeter of trees.

I now know that to move as fluidly as a cat in the darkness, it helps to have a cat's night vision, which I don't. So it was only a matter of time before I slammed into something. That wasn't what made the noise, though. It was the groan I let out when my forehead whacked the object I had slammed into — a tree. I froze and listened for some sign that Davis had heard me, but all I could hear was my own faint breath. After a moment, I inched forward. What I saw made me want to groan all over again.

Davis was standing on the back porch of the cottage, struggling with a sliding glass door, trying to jimmy it open. When that didn't work, he jumped down from the porch and shone his flashlight around. I ducked back into the trees and waited. In the distance I heard the hum of a car engine. It seemed to be approaching, then it faded altogether. It was probably way down on the main road. Or maybe it had gone to a nearby cottage. All I knew was that I didn't hear it anymore, so I didn't worry about it.

By the time I peeked out from the trees again, Davis had dragged a picnic table from somewhere and had positioned it under a window. He slung his backpack onto it and started to dig through it. He fished out something and climbed up onto the table. I gasped. The thing Davis had taken out of his backpack was a crowbar. He was using it to pry open the window. He was breaking into the place.

A jumble of thoughts tumbled through my mind. Had Davis broken into all of those other cottages? Was he wearing Nikes? I hadn't gotten a good look at his feet in the gym. If he was, would the soles match the print Levesque had managed to make from one of the break-in sites? Had Davis had anything to do with Stanley Meadows's death? I discarded the last question as soon as it popped into my mind. Davis was many things — pretentious, obnoxious and conceited were just three of his finer qualities that sprang to mind. But a killer? Get real! That didn't add up. Yet there he was, standing on a table trying to crowbar his way into a cottage to which he obviously did not have the key. No matter how you looked at it, this was not good.

Decision time. What should I do? I fingered the strap of my mini-knapsack. My camera was nestled inside, loaded and ready to shoot. What I ached to do was snap a picture of Davis breaking into the place. What stopped me was the simple fact of how my camera works. To get a picture, I'd have to use my flash. If the flash went off, Davis would see it. If he saw it . . . I thought it through. If he saw it and I didn't run fast enough, if he caught me, he could take the camera away from me. But unless he was ready to do some serious harm to me, he couldn't stop me from going to Steve Denby. He couldn't stop me from telling Steve what I had seen. And he sure couldn't stop Steve from investigating this break-in and comparing it to the others. I didn't even need to take a picture. I could go to Steve right now and tell him what I had seen. That way, Davis wouldn't be tipped off. He wouldn't have time to prepare any excuses. Steve would have the element of surprise working for him.

A loud *snap* made me jump. Davis had managed to pry the window open and was crawling through it. I told myself that I should back off out of earshot, dig out Phoebe's cell phone and call Steve Denby. But I couldn't tear myself away just yet. Davis had broken into a cottage. He had come prepared to do it and had known exactly how to get inside. That meant there was a pretty good chance that he had broken into those other cottages too. But why? Levesque had said that nothing valuable had been taken. Nothing that any of the owners had noticed and reported, anyway. Most of them had said they didn't keep anything of real value in their places. By the looks of it, this cottage was no exception. So why? Why was Davis breaking into places but taking nothing? I decided that I would call Steve as soon as I saw what he was doing.

I tiptoed through the darkness toward the cottage, keeping low, then crept up the steps of the porch and crouched to one side of the sliding glass door. My heart pounded in my chest. I told myself there was nothing to be afraid of. I wasn't doing anything wrong. Davis was. All I was going to do was take a quick look. With any luck, when I peeked in, I wouldn't come face to face with Davis peeking out.

I flattened myself on the floor of the porch with my head near the glass door and my feet nearly hanging off the edge. Then, sucking in a deep breath, I edged forward just far enough to catch a glimpse of the cottage interior.

At first I saw nothing. Then, off in one corner, I spotted the tell-tale ribbon of light. It took a moment for it all to come clear. Davis was sitting on a chair with his back to me. He was hunched over a desk. He held the flashlight in one hand. With the other hand, he was rooting through a drawer. What was he looking for? Money? Other small valuables? He slammed the top drawer shut and yanked open the next one. He worked quickly, rummaging through the contents. Then, suddenly, he sat up straight and snapped off the flashlight. I could barely make him out in there. He didn't seem to be moving. A thought jagged through my mind: He knows he's being watched! I jerked my head away from the glass door and pushed myself backward, meaning to wriggle off the porch, when the interior of the cottage suddenly lit up.

My heart stopped beating. Had he heard me? Did he know someone was out here? I held my breath and reminded myself that this was Davis. Even if he had somehow realized that he wasn't alone, he wasn't going to hurt me. He wouldn't dare. Then I heard a menacing growl, followed by a voice, one that wasn't Davis's. That's when I realized that I was the least of Davis's worries.

"What do you think you're doing?" the voice said. It came clearly through the window Davis had left open behind him. The owner of the cottage. It had to be.

"Gary," Davis said.

Gary? The same Gary I had seen at Davis's house? Davis had broken into Gary's place? Why?

"I asked you a question, Dave," Gary said. "Are you going to answer it, or do I take the muzzle off my friend here and let him persuade an answer out of you?"

I was dying to sneak another look, but I didn't dare, not with the lights on inside. I couldn't see what was going on, but, thanks to the open window, I could hear.

Davis laughed, but it came out dry and nervous, more like an edgy cackle than a good-humored guffaw.

"Geez, where did you come from? You startled me," Davis said. "Most dogs would have barked, given a guy a little warning."

"My dog isn't most dogs," Gary said. I remembered seeing him on the street with a nasty black beast that appeared to be part Rottweiler and part Satan. The dog growled again, a low, terrible rumble that sounded like it was coming from deep inside a beast the size of, say, *Tyrannosaurus Rex*. Then I heard a rattle, like a chain being yanked, and the dog fell silent. "I thought you would have figured that out by now. He doesn't have to make a lot of noise to tell me what he needs to tell me," Gary said. "And you haven't answered my question."

"I was waiting for you," Davis said. "I was hoping you'd turn up."

"Well, here I am," Gary said. "You think I'm stupid, Dave? Is that what you think?"

"No," he said. "I was just — "

"They're not here," Gary said.

Who — or what — wasn't there? What were they talking about?

"You were the one who took the first step," Gary said. "You wanted the inside story. Isn't that what you told me, Dave?"

Davis didn't say anything.

"And what did I tell you?"

Still nothing.

"What did I tell you?" Gary's voice was dangerously sharp.

Davis muttered something that I didn't catch.

"You're not bailing on me, Dave. You're not selling me out, not without making a whole lot of trouble for yourself. That's what those pictures were all about. Insurance."

Pictures. I remembered Davis standing at the foot of his driveway, looking at something in an envelope. I remembered him crouched down in his garage, burning what looked like a photograph. There was a lot more going on in Davis's life than I had suspected.

"Looks like keeping an eye on you was a good idea, Dave," Gary said. "You're in tight and you're in for good. If I even suspect that you're thinking of pulling something on me, I drop those pictures into the mail to the cops, you got me? Those nice, clear shots of you in all three places. Once they know you were in the first three, they're gonna pinch you for the other place."

The other place?

The Satan dog growled again, and again I heard the *chink-chink* of a chain, silencing him.

"You send those pictures," Davis said, "and you

get yourself in trouble, too."

"How do you figure that, Dave?"

"If you took the pictures, you had to be there."

I heard a low chuckle, the kind that sounded so cold that it made you want to pull on a sweater — right after you had a long, hot shower.

"I said I was gonna mail the photos, Dave. I don't have to stick around this dump town to do that. And maybe I need to remind you, but there's nothing, absolutely nothing to tie me to the last place. Far as anyone is ever going to know, that last place was your idea and you did it solo."

The other place? The *last* place? Stanley Meadows's place? I inched backwards. Time to run. Or, it would have been if my sweater hadn't caught on a nail, and if, while pulling so hard to get free, I hadn't whacked my head on one of the porch railings. It didn't exactly make a thundering sound, but it was loud enough that both Gary and Davis stopped talking. I jumped off the porch. Behind me, a dog barked. Barked, not growled. Barked loudly and savagely. I sprinted for the woods. I would have made it, too, if someone hadn't opened the sliding door and if something big and black and snarling hadn't hurtled at me. I heard it, I turned, and even in the darkness, I saw sharp, tearing teeth, unmuzzled and dripping with saliva. Then I heard the *fwoosh* of the glass door being slid wider.

"Take one more step," Gary said, "and I give him the attack order."

Chapter 14

Take one more step? Was Gary kidding? Like I could even move a muscle. That dog was big and mean-looking. It was the kind of dog you had to secure with a chain because it could chew through leather and nylon and rope the way I could chew through bread. The dog — the beast — crouched low, ready to fly through the air at me on command and bury its fangs in my neck. There should be a law against people keeping dogs like that.

I stared at the animal. Then I remembered something I'd seen in the dog book Mom insisted we all read after she had rescued Shendor on the highway and brought her home to join our family. Certain breeds of dogs — guard dogs and attack dogs (my knees almost buckled when those two words flashed across my brain, *attack dog*) — interpret direct eye contact as a challenge to their dominance. When their dominance is challenged, they'll fight to re-assert their superiority. I quickly averted my gaze.

"You know her?" Gary was saying.

I dared to turn my head only slightly and saw two figures silhouetted against the bright interior of the cottage. One of them nodded. Thanks a lot, Davis.

"She goes to my school," he said.

"What's she doing here?"

Davis shrugged.

"I was at a dance at school," I said, addressing Gary. "I was just going home. Taking a shortcut."

"A shortcut right up to my back door?" Gary said. He stepped out onto the porch.

"Her dad's the top cop in town," Davis said. Great. Double thanks a lot, Davis. Unless he meant it as a way to scare Gary into letting me go, in which case, thanks, Davis.

Gary didn't say anything.

"Hey, I'm sorry if I was trespassing," I said. "I live over that way." I raised a hand to point in the general direction of home. As soon as I did, the dog started growling and crouched even lower. I pulled my hand back slowly toward me. Make no threatening gestures. Make no sudden moves.

"Go get that flashlight," Gary said to Davis.

Davis obeyed. Gary turned the flashlight on me and took a good long look. The beam lingered on the rip in the front of my sweater. Then he swept the beam over the porch, stopping close to where I had been lying. He bent down, picked at something and held it in the beam for closer examination. Then he shone the light at my sweater again.

"She was up here on the porch," he said to Davis,

showing him what he had picked up. It was a little piece of red wool that had caught on the nail. "Come here," he said to me.

I stayed where I was. They suspected I had overheard what they'd said. If I went up there, nothing good was going to happen to me.

"Come here now," Gary said, "or I'll go inside and let Butcher play with you."

Butcher? Cute. I headed for the steps. When I got to the top, Gary grabbed me and shoved me inside. He yanked off my knapsack. Then he snapped his fingers and next thing I knew, Butcher was inside, too.

"Sit," Gary said. I didn't know if he was talking to me or the dog, so I dropped down onto the nearest chair, just to be on the safe side. Gary snapped his fingers again and Butcher rushed to his side. Gary bent down and said something low to the dog. Butcher sat, as relaxed as a coiled spring, watching me.

"You move," Gary said, as he closed and locked the sliding doors, "and, believe me, you'll never move again."

I believed him.

Gary and Davis went into another room. I sat trembling on the chair, not daring to look at Butcher, trying to beat back the waves of terror that were battering me. Think. Think. I should have cut out the minute I saw Davis slip through the window. I should have called Steve Denby and told him what I had seen. Should have, could have, would have. Useless words, right up there with *if only*. Words that changed nothing.

Think.

Gary and Davis had been involved in the death of Stanley Meadows, I was sure of that now. If they suspected that I knew, I was in big trouble. I should have gone to Toronto with Phoebe and Levesque. I should have stayed at the dance with Ross. I should have run the moment Davis pulled that crowbar from his backpack. Should have, could have, would have.

They were in the other room for only a few minutes, but it seemed a lot longer. Every breath I took sounded as loud as Darth Vader's breath to me. All I could think was that Butcher was a dog that could give in to his instincts at any second, and the second he did would be my last. I kept my head down, looking at his front paws, reassured that, so far, he had stayed exactly where Gary had put him. Good boy. Stay, boy.

I heard footsteps but didn't dare move. Gary and Davis came back into the room.

"Ten minutes," Gary was saying. "That's all it's going to take. You," he said to me, his voice sharp now. "Come here."

I kept my head low and looked at Butcher's paws again. Big, powerful paws. Paws that suddenly seemed as large as Levesque's feet. Slowly, careful not to alarm Butcher or threaten him in any way, I raised myself up off the chair. Gary grabbed my arm. His hand bit into my elbow as he shoved me ahead of him into a small room. Only after I was inside did he turn on the light. The room was windowless and empty except for a chair, a plastic garbage can, a couple of cardboard boxes, and a battered stool.

"You, too," Gary said to Davis. "No way I'm going to risk gassing up with the two of you in the car." Before he pushed Davis in with me, he patted him down and took away his cell phone. Geez. Two phones — Davis's and Phoebe's — both confiscated. They were turning out to be like cops — there was never one around when you needed it.

"Don't get any ideas," Gary said. "Butcher is going to be right outside this door. Even if you could get it open — which, trust me, you can't — you'll have to deal with him. And don't doubt it for a minute, this is a dog that's born to fight — and win. So play it smart, huh, Dave? I come back here and I see you sitting nice and quiet and we can figure out where to take it from there."

He grinned and stepped back across the threshold. The door closed and I heard a key turn in the lock. I breathed a sigh of relief. Butcher was out there. I was in here. It was a small thing, but it was the best thing that had happened to me all day.

For a while, neither of us said anything. We listened as Gary's footsteps grew fainter and fainter. We heard a car start somewhere outside. We heard the sound of its engine fade in the distance. I glanced around. The plastic garbage can was empty. I checked the cardboard boxes. Also empty. I threw one of them at the door just to see if Butcher was really there. Bad idea. Butcher growled and hurled himself against the door. The whole room shook. If he did that a couple more times, he'd splinter the wood and come sailing right on through. I was shaking as I waited to see if he'd keep battering at the door or if he'd give up. He gave up.

"Any more bright ideas?" Davis said. He was sitting on the floor, leaning against the wall, legs out in front of him.

"We have to get out of here, Davis," I said. But how? There was no window. The only door was guarded by good old Butcher. I looked at the chair and the stool. Maybe I could hide behind the door and hit Gary over the head with one of them when he came back — assuming Davis cooperated. But if I did, there'd be no one to call off Butcher. I didn't know what the dog was trained to do if anyone attacked his master, and I sure didn't want to find out.

Davis dropped his head down onto his knees. "You should have kept out of this," he said.

"I didn't know what *this* was, Davis."

"Then what are you doing here?"

"It's all your fault," I said. I told him I knew he had been behind forging my handwriting and that I'd followed him because I thought he was going to get me into trouble again and I wanted to catch him red-handed.

"Yeah, well, congratulations, Sherlock," he said. "You caught me."

I looked at the locked door. "What do you think he's going to do to us?"

Davis's head bobbed up again. "To us?" he said. "Nothing. To you? You really stepped in it, Chloe. In case you hadn't noticed, Gary's not a nice guy."

My stomach felt like it was home to the Cirque de Soleil. A dog named Butcher was standing guard over me until a creep named Gary returned, and an idiot named Davis, who was mixed up in something bad, was trying to stonewall me. If I had gone to Toronto with Phoebe and Levesque, I'd be safe in a hotel by now.

"How did you get involved with Gary?"

Nothing. Davis stared at the wall opposite him.

"Geez, Davis — "

"I was working on this screenplay so I can get into the CFI," he said. "I had this dynamite idea — "

"What? How to get away with murder?"

He gave me a withering look. "It's about alienated youth," he said.

"Sarah said it was about a thief."

"That, too," Davis said. "Anyway, I was wandering around out here and I saw someone's place. A summer place. The window was open a little." He hesitated and glanced at me. "I decided to go in."

"Break in, you mean?"

"I already told you, the window was open."

"Oh, well, that makes it all right then."

"What is it with you?" he said angrily. "You've

only got one act, right? Sarcasm."

"Sorry," I said. I wasn't.

"I just wanted to see what a thief might feel like being in someone's place — alone." He shook his head. "Then, not long after that, I ran into Gary. I was really surprised to see him up here."

"You know him from somewhere else?"

"I met him in Toronto when I was doing that series on street kids. I used to see him and his dog downtown all the time. He's pretty cool."

"A real Tony Soprano," I said

Davis shrugged. "He was into stuff. So what?"

"What do you mean, stuff?"

"People said he did B and E's. They said he was good. Anyway, we got talking and I told him what I was working on. He was really interested, you know. He offered to show me a few things, give me a few ideas for my script."

"And you said yes?"

Davis nodded.

I wanted to scream. I was locked in this room, being guarded by a killer dog because some rich city kid had gone looking for a Quentin Tarantino moment and had messed up.

"Verisimilitude," I said. "It's a concept you should explore."

"Huh?"

"It is possible to write about criminals without actually committing a crime, Davis. You don't have to *do* the real thing. You just have to make it seem real."

"We never took anything," he said. "We just went inside and looked around. You ever been inside a place when no one's home? A complete stranger's place? It's amazing! And you can learn things about people by the kind of stuff they leave lying around. You know, magazines you find stashed under a guy's bed or little secrets in Mom or Dad's bedside table."

I sort of knew what he meant. I had felt a thrill when I was following him, watching him when he didn't know he was being watched. But I wasn't going to tell him that.

"Invasion of privacy as an entertainment option," I said.

He shot me another irritated look. "I thought it would give me insight."

"Into what?"

"Into the mind of the petty criminal," he said.

The Tarantino thing again.

I thought about Gary and Butcher. I thought about Gary returning with his car gassed up. I thought about what would happen after that. I started to shake all over.

"We have to get out of here, Davis."

He said nothing.

"What makes you sure he's not going to do anything to *you?*" I said. "He caught you breaking in here."

"He's already got me good," he said. He didn't sound happy about it, and if he was as panicky as I was about what might or might not happen next, he gave no sign of it. Mostly he sounded resigned. "You heard what he said — and don't even bother pretending that you didn't. He wasn't even in the place."

He didn't say what place. He didn't have to. I know he meant Stanley Meadows's place.

"What's in those pictures, Davis?"

No response.

"Davis, he's going to come back here. I have a feeling that's not going to be a good thing for me. I also have a feeling that you're going to let him do whatever it is he's planning to do. You owe it to me to at least tell me what this is all about."

For a few heartbeats, nothing. Then, "He said he wanted to make sure that if he showed me how to do it — "

"How to break in?"

He nodded. "He wanted some guarantee that I wouldn't rat him out. So he took pictures of me in the places we broke into. That way, if I told anyone, he had proof that I was there too."

That showed that Gary's brain was in good working condition, but it didn't say much about Davis's. Then again, breaking and entering wasn't exactly brilliant.

"What happened at Meadows's place?" I asked.

Davis turned his head away from me. I heard gulping sounds. Before he turned to face me again, he wiped a hand roughly across his face.

"I wasn't going to do it again. After three times, I figured I knew everything there was to know.

Besides, it was starting to get boring."

I waited.

"Then Gary said he had something special he wanted to show me. He said it would be a real kick. He told me where to meet him."

"Which was . . . ?"

"Around the back of the place."

"Meadows's cottage?"

He nodded. "Gary was there, waiting for me. He had scouted out the place. He always scouted them out. Then he said, 'Okay, this one's yours.'"

"Meaning?"

"Meaning he was going to let me do the actual work." Since when was breaking in considered work? "I was going to go in first, too." He peered at the wall opposite him again as he continued his story. "So I did it. I thought it would be cool, you know?" Actually, I didn't. "I went to the back window. I got it open. I started to crawl through. Just before I did, Gary slipped me something."

A gun, I thought.

"A gun," he said.

"Geez, Davis!" I mean, how stupid did you have to be?

"You ever held a gun?"

I shook my head. Levesque's gun was around the house a lot, but he'd made it clear what would happen to anyone who touched it. I get into enough trouble as it is.

"They're heavier than you think they're going to be," Davis said. "Sturdier, you know? The only gun

I ever held before was a toy gun when I was a kid. When Gary handed me this one, I almost dropped it. Gary thought that was pretty funny. 'Take it,' he said. 'It'll make you feel like the genuine article. Isn't that what you want, Dave? Don't you want to be the genuine article?'"

"Do you have any idea how serious that is, breaking and entering with a gun?"

He gave me a weary look. If he hadn't known when he entered Stanley Meadows's cottage, he sure did now.

"The place was dark, just like every other place we'd been in. I got inside. Then, all of a sudden, I heard something. A noise, like there was someone else in the house, only there couldn't have been because Gary was still outside somewhere. Then this shape appeared in a doorway. A guy. He had a shotgun or something. And it was pointed right at me. He didn't say, 'Stop or I'll shoot.' He didn't say anything. He just pointed the thing at me and he aimed and — "

"You shot him?"

"He was going to *kill* me. He wasn't going to warn me first or anything. The guy was going to kill me. So, yeah, I panicked and shot. I wasn't sure I was even going to hit him, but I've got to tell you, I was hoping. Man, was I hoping!"

"It could have been self-defense," I said. "Except for the fact that the guy was killed protecting his property from an armed intruder."

"Those pictures tie me to every other place we

broke into," Davis said.

"And Gary probably wasn't anywhere near Meadows's place any longer, let alone inside it, when you shot Meadows."

Davis nodded. "You see my problem," he said.

I also saw my own problem pretty clearly.

"You could have told the cops," I said.

"Right," Davis said, without conviction.

We sat in silence for a few moments, each lost in our own thoughts. Gary would be back soon. Then what? He knew I had heard too much. He'd want to get me out of the way. And what about Davis? Was he also a problem or was he the best alibi Gary had?

"This guy Meadows," I said, "where did he come from?"

"What do you mean?"

"You said he appeared out of nowhere. Where do you think he came from?"

Davis shrugged. "How should I know? He was just there."

"You didn't hear him drive up?"

"No."

"So you think he was in the cottage the whole time?"

"He must have been. Geez, Gary really screwed up when he scouted out the place."

That was one theory.

"You knew Meadows was hiding out up here, right?" I said.

This earned me a flicker of interest.

"He was supposed to testify against his business partner," I said. "Only now he's conveniently dead."

"What are you saying?"

"His car was in the garage, Davis."

He stared silently at me, his face completely blank, as if I hadn't spoken at all.

"His car was in the garage next to the house," I said. "If Gary scouted out the place, then he must have seen the car. If he saw the car, then he must have known that someone was home. Or that someone was around and could walk into the house at any moment. There weren't any cars at any of the other places you broke into. When cottages are empty, cars are gone."

"So?" Davis said. But I could tell by the horror blossoming in his eyes that he had mostly figured it out.

"I'm saying that maybe you were set up."

He shook his head, the way you do when you're sure you aced an exam and you get the exam paper back and there's a great big red F scrawled across the first page.

"Think about it, Davis. If Meadows drove up just before you went into the house or while you were inside, you would have heard him. The driveway is gravel. It makes a lot of noise when a car drives over it. So he must have been in the cottage when you broke in. That means that his car was in the garage. Are you going to tell me that when Gary scouted out the place before you got there, he didn't check out the garage?"

Left, right, left, right. Davis's head swung slowly back and forth.

"Three break-ins with no gun, and all of a sudden Gary hands you one and lets you go all by yourself into a cottage where there's a guy who's hiding out because he's scheduled to testify against his business partner and he's afraid of what might happen to him if anyone finds out where he is. That doesn't strike you as kind of funny? And there's nothing to tie Gary to the place, right? There's just a pattern of break-ins and a set of pictures of you in every place that was broken into. Geez, Davis, why don't you just paint a big target on your chest?"

His eyes grew wider as he digested all of this.

"We have to get out of here before Gary comes back," I said.

"I killed the guy." His voice was flat, dead.

"We have to go to the police. You have to tell them exactly what happened."

"I killed the guy," he said again. "I can't — "

I heard a sound, a sort of purr. Then a car door opened and closed. Gary.

"Davis, you have to help me."

The shake of his head was slow, but steady.

"I can't," he said. "I'm in too deep."

Chapter 15

In the next few seconds, I heard a lifetime's worth of sounds. Footsteps on the cottage's porch. A key in a lock. The sigh of a door opening and the slam of it closing again. A dog's toenails first on a wood floor, then on linoleum. Gary's voice, soft, cooing at a dog named Butcher. My heart, pounding in my chest. The whisper of a prayer.

I looked at Davis. He refused to meet my eyes. He sat on the floor, his legs drawn up to his chest, his arms wrapped around his knees. I stared at him, but I wasn't thinking about him. There was one thing and one thing only in my mind — a single word, gigantic and flashing like a signal in the dark: DANGER.

A few moments — a few hours? — passed before Gary unlocked the door to the small room where Davis and I waited. Davis jumped up when he heard the key slide into the lock. He shook himself, like he was trying to shake off dirt or muddy water or the stink of something bad. The sick, worried look disappeared from his face. He looked cool again, composed, a guy dressed in black who would have slid on his sunglasses if it wasn't nighttime.

The door swung open and Butcher lunged into the room. Gary grabbed the chain around his neck and yanked him back. He smiled at me.

"I hear your daddy's out of town," he said. "In fact, your whole family's out of town. Won't be back until, what, sometime Sunday?"

What genius had told him that?

"Two days is a long time," he said. "Plenty of time for a girl to get herself into a whole pile of trouble."

"You sure that's such a good idea?" Davis said. "She's a cop's kid."

As if that were the only reason that hurting me was a bad idea.

"When papa's away," Gary said.

The rats will play, I thought.

"The junior cop was at the gas station. I overheard him talking to the old geezer who runs the place. The head honcho is down in Toronto on family business. We're in the clear."

"Yeah, but — "

"Don't stress, Dave," Gary said pleasantly. He looked relaxed, like a guy who'd just returned from a three-week vacation or a three-hour massage. "She's just gonna disappear, that's all. There's plenty of space up here for a person to go missing. Isn't that right, Dave?"

Say no. Make it hard for him, Davis.

Davis nodded.

"And you're going to take care of it, right, Dave?" Gary said. "Because you have a lot to lose, my friend. She tells Daddy what she knows, and you can kiss your butt goodbye, you know what I mean?"

Davis said nothing.

"Be a good boy, Dave. Do as you're told and those photos won't find their way into the wrong hands. First she disappears, then I disappear and I stay disappeared as long as you keep your mouth shut. Remember, all I did was break into a couple of places. I didn't take anything — except those pictures, of course. I never even set foot in the last place." He grinned. "You wash my back, I wash yours. Nice, neat, simple."

Davis didn't return the smile. He didn't protest, either. "What do you have in mind?" he said.

Gary shrugged. "I was thinking maybe a nice walk in the woods. Someplace out of the way. Someplace nobody would think to look." He handed me my mini-knapsack, even helped me slip my arms through the straps. "I don't want any loose ends," he said, smiling. "Oh, and your phone? Something seems to be wrong with it. It just stopped working."

He tossed a piece of nylon rope to Davis. "Make it tight, Dave. I'm gonna check. I don't give out merit badges, but I can get real heavy with the demerit points, if you follow me."

Davis caught the rope and nodded at me to turn around. When I hesitated, Gary loosened his grip on Butcher. I turned.

Maybe in a previous life, Davis had been a boy scout. He sure knew his knots.

"Nice," Gary said, yanking at the rope. He produced a rag from somewhere, twisted it and used it to gag me. Then he said, "Come on."

Butcher growled.

When we got outside, I was surprised to see that the black sky was strewn with stars. The night air was clear and fresh and smelled of trees in early bud. I breathed in deeply and was rewarded with the scent of pine and spruce, fragrances I might have appreciated if I hadn't been so terrified.

Gary nudged me toward a car parked on the gravel in front of the cottage. He opened one of the back doors and gestured for me to get inside. When I didn't move — I couldn't move, couldn't make myself move because I knew if I took a ride in that car, I'd never take another ride again — Gary gave Butcher's leash a little slack to prod me along. Quaking, nauseous, fighting back tears, I struggled into the back seat as best as I could with my arms pinned behind my back. Gary tossed the car keys to Davis. Then he opened the front passenger door and fastened Butcher's chain to the headrest.

"Get in," Gary said to Davis. "And, remember, I'll be right behind you." He opened his jacket to reveal the butt of a gun poking out of his belt.

Davis didn't argue. I hoped that whatever happened to him during the rest of his life would be seriously unpleasant. I hoped it even more fervently when, standing out there in the night, under the Big Dipper, a set of car keys in his hand, he said, "I know a place."

Silence.

"A real good place for a person to disappear," he said. "No one ever goes there."

Gary was smiling as he climbed into the back seat beside me.

* * *

I sat in the car, staring at the back of Davis's head and thinking about every movie I had ever seen where some poor guy is about to disappear for good. Thinking how if I had known then what I knew now, I never would have watched those movies because what did they know about what it was really like? My hands were tied behind me, out of Gary's sight. I twisted my fingers to claw at the rope. The knot felt funny. It wasn't a reef knot, I knew that much. But I couldn't loosen it.

Davis backed the car down the gravel driveway as carefully as if he were chauffeuring his grandmother to church on a Sunday morning. Then he swung east.

"By the book," Gary warned him. "No speeding, no funny business."

Annoyance flickered in Davis's eyes as he glanced at Gary in the rearview mirror.

"You think I want to get nailed?" Davis said. "You think I'm ready to call it quits on my life?"

That must have been exactly what Gary wanted to hear, because he settled into the seat beside me.

"Where are we going?" he asked.

"The perfect place," Davis said. "A place I found."

He drove around the south end of the park and then headed north, along its eastern perimeter. Eventually he turned west again, and guided the car off the main road and onto what was little more than a dirt track. He pulled into the trees and killed the engine.

Gary got out of the car.

"Pop the trunk," he said.

I heard a dull *ka-chonk* as Gary reached into the car and yanked me out. He held fast to the rope that bound my hands while he lifted the trunk lid and pulled out a flashlight. He switched it on. I heard the driver's door open and turned to see Davis's dark form.

"We have to go a ways into the woods," Davis said. "It's not far."

Gary was still rummaging in the trunk. At first I didn't see what he was pulling out. Then he called to Davis. "Catch!"

In the flashlight's beam I saw a shovel sail through the air. Davis caught it handily. I froze in horror. Gary slammed the trunk shut. He had another length of rope in his hands and was tying a knot in the middle of it. I frowned at first. What was he . . . ? Then I started to shake all over again. Gary grabbed me by one arm and hauled me around to the front passenger door, opened it, and reached for Butcher's chain to loosen it.

"Uh-uh," Davis said.

"What do you mean, uh-uh?" Gary said.

"You want me to do this, I do it without that dog snapping at my butt," Davis said. "He stays in the car."

Gary hesitated.

"You want me to be nervous?" Davis said. "You want to have to do this yourself, get your hands all dirty?"

Gary fingered the gun in his belt. "Sorry, boy," he murmured to Butcher, before slamming the car door. Then, "Which way?" as the door locks automatically engaged. Butcher was locked in. Under different circumstances, I would have been thrilled.

Davis had taken his own small flashlight out of his pocket. He shone it to his right.

"There's an old trail," he said.

Maybe it was panic, but it took me a few moments to work out what Davis apparently already knew. The city boy was full of surprises. He had guided Gary to the most deserted place in the park and he had done it in the dead of night. The trail he was indicating led to Puzzle Rock.

Davis took the lead. Gary nudged me along ahead of him. We walked slowly along an overgrown trail until, finally, we reached the outcropping of limestone rock. The beam of Gary's flashlight danced over it. He grunted.

"You sure this is a good place?" he said.

Davis nodded. "I told you, nobody comes here. A kid fell off the cliff up there a few years back and almost got killed." I would have been impressed at the effort he'd put into his homework, if it wasn't for everything else he had done. "It's off limits."

My whole body started to tingle. I had the oddest feeling that it didn't belong to me anymore, that it was nothing more than a suit of clothes I was wearing, something I could shuck off at any time. I floated along in that suit of clothes, Davis in front of me, Gary behind me, and I wondered, almost idly, the way you wonder what your mom's planning for supper, whether Davis was planning to shove me off the top of Puzzle Rock. I don't know how far we walked or how fast. It seemed like no time at all, and all night. Then the beam of Davis's flashlight cut through the night and I saw the gnarled root of a cedar tree clinging like a toe to a mammoth slab of limestone. We were there.

"No one will ever look here," Davis said. He shoved me toward the sheer face of limestone.

A second flashlight beam scanned the area. "A person could have a nasty fall from up there," Gary said. The idea seemed to please him. I don't know what Davis had in mind when he brought me here, but I didn't have to be a mind reader to figure out what Gary had planned.

"A person could definitely have a nasty fall," Davis said. "It could even look like an accident, which would make everyone's life easier."

Everyone's life except mine.

Davis suddenly let out a shout and lunged toward me.

"What the . . . ?" he yelled. "There's something there."

"What?" Gary said. He didn't seem so relaxed now. The beam of his flashlight swung away from Puzzle Rock and cut into the night behind Davis.

Then a bunch of things happened all at once. First, something yanked so hard on my wrists that my arms were almost ripped from their sockets. Then, I don't even know how, my hands were free of the rope and something was being shoved into one of them. Something metallic. Something shaped like a cylinder. Then someone pushed me hard, propelling me toward Puzzle Rock.

"Go!" a voice hissed.

The cylinder was a small flashlight, the same one Davis had used to get to Gary's cottage. I flicked it on as I ran toward Puzzle Rock and scanned it for that familiar place. Behind me, I heard Davis cry out in what sounded like pain. Gary-inflicted pain? I'd no idea. I ran. At first I thought I'd never find the mark that indicated the entrance. I wished I had made it bigger. Then, suddenly, there it was. I switched off my flashlight and ran toward it in the dark. I stopped for a split second once I was inside so I could hear what was going on behind me. I saw a flashlight beam dance on the wall just behind me, but it didn't touch me. It couldn't touch me. I was in too deep.

"What's going on? What happened?" Gary was shouting. "If you — "

"I don't *know!*" Davis's voice sounded panicky.

"Something came at me. Did you see it?"

"Where's the girl?"

"I think she went that way," Davis said. I didn't know where he was pointing and didn't hang around to find out.

"Give me the car keys," Gary said.

"Geez," Davis gasped.

"What?"

"I think I left them in the car door."

Gary yelled. Davis apologized.

"Where are you going?" Davis said.

"Where do you think I'm going? Back to the car to get Butcher. You better pray, Dave. You better pray she doesn't get away."

I didn't know about Davis, but I was praying precisely the opposite. I wound my way through Puzzle Rock as fast as I could. I didn't pause for even a second to figure out what was going on behind me, I just ran. As I came out the other side I thought I heard something snarl in the distance. Butcher? No, Gary couldn't have gotten back to the car so fast. I must have imagined it. But I made a gold medal sprint through the trees, moving, moving, gasping, running until my knees screamed and my lungs felt as if they would explode. I heard more shouting behind me. Gary, I think, but I wasn't positive. Then I exploded out of the park. The railroad tracks were just ahead of me and beyond them about half a mile was my house. As I sprinted across the open ground I realized that except for the pounding of my feet on the

194

hard earth and my heart in my chest, everything seemed quiet. The calm before the storm?

I cleared the railroad tracks and crossed open field. There were houses in the distance. One of them was mine. I ran toward it. The whole time I was moving I was expecting Butcher to leap through the air behind me and sink his teeth into the back of my neck. My house got closer and closer. The whole rest of the world fell away. There was nothing but my house. Sturdy. Safe. I was across the road from it. I was on the driveway. I was on the porch. I was hunting through my mini-knapsack with trembling fingers. Keys. Keys! Oh *please* let there be keys. My fingers closed on metal. I yanked my keys out and sorted through them. There were only three of them, but it took me five tries to get the right one in the lock. Inside, Shendor was barking and scratching at the door. Then, I could hardly believe it, I was inside and Shendor was jumping up on me, glad to see me. I was even gladder to see her. I locked the door and ran to the kitchen for the phone.

I dialed Levesque's cell number. I didn't care that he was hundreds of miles away. I dialed it and when I heard his voice I started to shake so badly I thought I was going to pass out. I spilled out my story.

"Hang up," he said.

I couldn't move.

"*Hang up,* Chloe. I'm going to call Steve and then

I'm going to call you right back. Do you understand?"

I nodded.

"Chloe?"

"Yes," I said. "I understand."

Even after everything I had been through that night, hanging up that phone was the hardest thing I had ever done. But I did it and then I sat down in the middle of the kitchen floor, straining to hear the sounds of the night, the sounds of danger. Shendor dropped down onto the floor beside me and plunked her head down into my lap. She was warm and comforting. When the phone rang a few moments later, I just about jumped out of my skin. So did Shendor.

"You okay?" Levesque said.

I managed a pitiful "Yes," then I put my hand over the mouthpiece so that he wouldn't hear that I had started to cry.

"Steve's on his way over," Levesque said. "I'm going to stay on the line with you until he gets there. And I called the OPP detachment down in Carlisle. They're going to send some officers up there. It's going to be okay."

"But Davis — "

"One thing at a time," Levesque said. "Okay?"

"Okay," I said. My voice was shaking.

"Talk to me, Chloe. Tell me about that history essay you wrote."

Huh?

"What was it on again?"

"Les filles du roi," I told him.

"Oh, yeah. Young girls shipped over from France to marry the fur traders and *habitants* in New France, right? How many came over?"

I told him. With his coaxing, I told him everything I knew about the subject. It passed the time until the doorbell rang.

"Someone's here," I said into the phone.

"Chloe?" a voice called. Steve Denby's voice.

"It's Steve," I said into the phone.

"Let him in."

I carried the phone with me to the door and peeked out through the window. It really was Steve. I unlocked the door to let him in. I felt like hugging him.

"Are you okay?" he said.

I nodded. A distant voice came from the phone in my hand. I held it to my ear, then I handed it over to Steve.

"He wants to talk to you," I said.

Steve listened to the phone for a few moments, then he stepped into the kitchen.

"They're on their way," he said to Levesque. Then, "Don't worry. She stays with me until we get this sorted out." Then, "I will." He hung up and turned back to me. "Come on," he said. "I'm taking you into town. You can tell me everything on the way."

I told him what had happened from the time I decided to follow Davis to the time I was running for my life.

"It was Davis," I said. "He shot Stanley Meadows."

I wondered where he was now. I wondered if Gary had figured out that Davis had helped me escape. If so, what had he done to Davis? I wondered if I would ever see him and his stupid sunglasses again.

Chapter 16

An OPP cruiser was pulling up in front of the police station just as we arrived. Steve made me get out of the car and told me to go into the police station while he went to talk to the OPP officers. I looked at the OPP car and thought I saw someone in the back seat, but I wasn't sure. I went inside and huddled in Levesque's chair, wishing I had brought a jacket with me. I kept thinking about Gary and Butcher. I had been close — too close. If Davis hadn't changed his mind at the last minute, if we hadn't been at Puzzle Rock, if I hadn't told Davis what I knew about Puzzle Rock, if, if, if . . .

The door to the police station opened. Steve and the OPP officers came in. They had someone with them.

Davis didn't look too good. The knees of his black jeans were smudged with dirt. One elbow of his leather jacket was badly scuffed. His hair was standing up in all directions. A cut ran across one swollen cheek. His eyes went straight to me and he nodded. I found out later that he had flagged down the OPP cruiser on the highway.

Steve sat him down and let him call his mother. She showed up a little later. She and Davis disappeared into a room with Steve and one of the OPP officers. It wasn't long before the OPP officer emerged to confer with his colleague, then they left. I heard their car drive away.

I was alone at Levesque's desk for nearly an hour before Steve reappeared.

"This is going to take a while, Chloe," he said. "You want me to call someone? Maybe you could stay with a friend for a while?"

I shook my head. "I'm okay here," I said. Nobody had said where Gary and Butcher were, so I assumed they were still out there somewhere. If he was out there, then I wanted to be in here, in the police station.

Steve didn't argue with me. He disappeared again. I glanced around. There was a half a pot of coffee on a hot plate. I had no idea how long it had been there and I didn't care. I got up and poured myself a cup. As I carried it back to where I had been sitting, I passed Steve's desk. The plastic envelope containing the page from the *Oxford Canadian Dictionary* was sitting on the top of his IN basket. Right next to it, with yellow notes sticking out in a dozen places, was his book on fingerprints. I picked it up and carried it back to Levesque's desk. It would give me something to do while I waited. Waited for what, though, I wasn't sure.

I flipped through the book. Butcher's snarling

face looked out at me from the first fifty or so pages. Then, suddenly, he wasn't there anymore. Maybe that was because Steve was in the next room, and he had a gun and knew how to use it. Or maybe it was because I was sitting in Levesque's chair. Slowly, I started to feel safe.

I was staring at a page-long explanation of the merits of something called ninhydrin when Mom, Levesque and Phoebe walked in. I checked the clock on the wall. It was that part of the night that Mom calls the wee hours of the morning. They must have gotten in the car the minute I called. They must have driven straight through. Mom was all over me, hugging me, before I knew what was happening. "We were so worried. Louis was pulled over on the way back. He would have gotten a speeding ticket if he hadn't shown his police identification."

Mr. Law and Order was speeding on my account?

"You okay?" Levesque asked. He inspected me closely even after I said that I was fine. Then he went to confer with Steve.

I put Steve's book back on his desk and went home with Mom and Phoebe. I was pretty sure I wasn't going to be able to sleep. I was wrong.

I woke up at nine the next morning. The door to Mom's bedroom was open. She was still sleeping. Levesque was gone. When I saw that he wasn't downstairs, I headed out to find him.

* * *

Levesque had his feet up on his desk. He was leaning back in his chair, cradling a cup of coffee in his hands. He actually smiled when he saw me.

"You're up early for a Saturday," he said.

"And you're looking pretty relaxed considering someone tried to kill me last night."

"Well, he won't be doing that again any time soon."

"I mean Gary," I said.

"So do I. I just got a call from the OPP. They picked him up — " He consulted his watch. "A few hours ago."

"You sure it's him?"

He nodded. "Gary Leaming. He has a record."

"For murder?"

Levesque shook his head. "Burglary."

"He set Davis up, didn't he?"

At first Levesque said nothing. Then he nodded. "Looks that way. It wouldn't have happened, though, if Davis hadn't gone looking for trouble."

No kidding.

"Gary wasn't actually counting on someone like Davis to come along, was he?" I said. "He didn't come up here looking for someone to kill Meadows for him."

Levesque shook his head. "From what I hear, he isn't quite that stupid. He was up here to make sure Meadows didn't make it to court to testify. Davis was just a bonus for him, a way to keep himself removed from the actual killing. If Davis hadn't stumbled into it, Gary would have taken care of business all by himself."

Something was still bothering me. Actually, a lot of things were still bothering me.

"So Davis comes along," I said. It was all falling into place now. "He runs into Gary and starts bragging to him about breaking into a cottage. Then he starts telling Gary about his screenplay — "

"And Gary suggests he could show Davis a few things," Levesque said. "At least, that's what Davis says."

"So those first break-ins, the ones with nothing taken?"

"Those incriminated Davis. Gary took pictures to make sure of that. He also made sure we'd find out about the break-ins, which established a pattern — that way we'd think Meadows was killed by the same person, as part of another break-in."

"But most of the cottages up here aren't occupied this time of year. How could he be sure you'd find out?"

"I suspect he reported the first one himself," Levesque said. I thought back to Sunday dinner. Levesque had said the first break-in had been reported by a guy who was out walking his dog.

"And the other two?"

"The hiking club advertises its route. I figure that all Gary had to do was pick a place that could be easily seen from the trail. And the handyman who discovered the third break-in spends a lot of evenings down at Ralph's. Davis says that Gary did, too."

I nodded again, remembering when I had gone

there to interview the football team for my article on the cafeteria menu. Davis had appeared. He had been looking for someone.

"Why didn't Gary just take off as soon as Meadows was dead, though?" I asked. "Why did he stick around for three days?"

Levesque shrugged. "That I won't know until Gary makes a full statement. But I'd guess it's because he got a little nervous about what Davis might do. Implicating someone in a murder might have seemed like a good idea, but it created a whole new set of problems for Gary."

"What's going to happen to Davis?"

"I'd say he's gotten himself into a fair amount of trouble."

"He did save my life," I said.

Levesque did not soften in the slightest. "But first he put it in jeopardy."

* * *

The first person I met when I left the police station was Ross. He wanted the whole story. I promised to tell it to him under two conditions. One, that he buy me breakfast — well, brunch really — at Stella's Great Home Cooking. Two, that he promise not to tell a soul what I was going to tell him.

I was just polishing off the last bite of my cheese omelet when Daria entered the restaurant. She stood at the door and looked around. Then her eyes lit on me. As she strode toward me, I braced myself.

"I have to talk to you," she said.

I picked up the polished metal napkin holder

that was on the table and peered into it. "Well, what do you know," I said to Ross. "I'm not invisible anymore."

Daria's cheeks turned pink. "I really have to talk to you," she said.

I waved her into the seat opposite me. After all, she had saved me from getting into trouble with Ms. Jeffries after Mr. Green found his paper in my things. I wanted to hear why.

Ross started to slide out of the booth.

"You can stay," I told him. To Daria I said, "Ross is my friend."

That didn't scare her away. She slid onto the bench next to him.

"All the things that happened to Mr. Green's car?" she said, and paused. Was she asking me something or telling me something? "It was Rick," she said finally. "The forgery, that was Davis's doing. Sarah told me about it. She felt guilty. I told Rick. I wasn't supposed to. I wasn't supposed to tell anyone." But she had. "As soon as I told him, I could see the wheels turning in his head. The punctured tire, the theft from Mr. Green's car, slipping Mr. Green's paper into your binder — "

"How did he do that, anyway?"

"Remember the fight in the hallway that morning?"

I did.

"Notice anything about the two guys involved?"

I started to shake my head. They were just two guys. Two guys from the football team . . . "Oh," I said.

"It was all Rick."

I didn't even have to ask why.

"I wasn't there when he did it and I didn't have anything to do with it. But he told me. And, like a fool, I kept my mouth shut."

"Until Mr. Green's paper fell out of my binder."

She shrugged. "Enough is enough," she said. "I'm going to Ms. Jeffries first thing Monday morning to tell her everything. Not that it's going to do a lot of good. Rick will deny it and I can't prove anything. It'll be my word against his."

I thought about that for a few minutes. Maybe she was right. Maybe not.

"Daria? What if I knew a way so that it wasn't his word against yours?"

She looked interested.

"You might want to hold off on talking to Ms. Jeffries though," I said.

Now she looked *really* interested.

* * *

I had trouble sleeping that night. Twice I fell asleep and twice I woke up in the middle of a nightmare in which I was being chased by a savage dog named Butcher. The first time he was rocketing toward me, razor-sharp teeth bared and ready to tear and rip. The second time, he actually buried his teeth in my shoulder. I woke up with a dry mouth, damp cheeks and a hammering heart. I got out of bed, went downstairs, turned on the TV low and settled down on the couch to watch reruns of stupid reruns from a few decades ago. Cheesy as they were, they were better than the movie that had been looping in my head.

Somewhere between four-thirty and five in the morning, Mom crept down the stairs. Her hair was sticking up all over her head. She came and sat down beside me.

"Did the TV wake you up?" I said.

She shook her head. "I just woke up and had this crazy urge to check on you. I went to peek in your room." She laughed. "I haven't done that in years."

"Well, I'm fine," I told her.

She sat with me for a while. We watched an old *Jack Benny Show*. It was actually pretty funny. Then Mom made me a mug of hot chocolate. After I drank it, she made me go upstairs to bed. I woke up in time for Sunday dinner.

"Any news on Davis?" I asked, as I passed the potatoes to Levesque.

He shrugged. "The Crown hasn't sorted out the charges yet. There are the break and enters, for sure. Maybe a weapons charge. Manslaughter, maybe. His father has apparently hired a high-priced lawyer. And he is a minor. Under the circumstances, I guess he could argue that he was tricked into participating in the break and enter at Meadows's place and that he shot Meadows in self-defense. I don't think that would work if it had been Gary who had done the shooting. But it's clear Davis was manipulated. He knew what he was doing was wrong, but he didn't know what he was getting into."

"He *was* asking for trouble," Phoebe said.

"There's no doubt about that," Levesque said, passing her the potatoes. "At issue is precisely how much trouble he was asking for."

"What if it had happened the other way?" I asked. "Meadows was hiding out. He had a gun himself. Even if he wasn't expecting something to happen that night, he was prepared just in case it did. Davis said that Meadows didn't warn him, didn't say, 'Stop or I'll shoot.' He just raised his gun and it looked like he was going to fire, so Davis shot him. But what if Davis had missed? What if Meadows had shot Davis instead?"

"I can't speak for Gary," Levesque said, after a few moments, "but I know what I would have done."

We all waited.

"Shoot Meadows with Davis's gun," my mother said, just like that. We all stared at her, Levesque harder than Phoebe and I. Mom's cheeks turned red. "Well, that would have worked, wouldn't it? It would have looked like Meadows had surprised a burglar and that they had shot each other. Wouldn't it?"

"Yes," Levesque agreed. "That would have worked. But I'm not sure I like the amount of thought my family gives to criminal activity."

Mom turned even pinker and smiled until it looked like her face was going to split. I think it was the word "family" that did it.

"So, all things considered," I said, "I guess Davis

is lucky." I wondered if he saw it that way, though.

* * *

I had to wait until Monday morning on my way to school to connect with Steve Denby again. I asked him to explain to me about ninhydrin. Then I also quizzed him about paper. It turned out that I had understood what I had read in his fingerprint book while I'd been waiting for Levesque and Mom and Phoebe to return from Toronto. After I talked to Steve, I had to do some more waiting. Until lunchtime, to be precise.

Rick and Daria were occupying their own booth at Ralph's. Rick was eating a burger and fries. Daria just had a plate of fries. They each had a glass of Coke in front of them. Rick's was half-empty. Daria spotted me and nodded almost imperceptibly.

"Hey, Rick," I said, sliding into the booth beside her.

"I heard you came close to being dog food," he said, through a mouthful of burger.

"Yeah? Well, I heard the cops found the tool that was used to break into Mr. Green's car and that they've tested it for fingerprints. And, guess what, they found one. A nice clean one."

Rick took a sip of his Coke, then another bite of his burger.

"So?" he said.

"So," I said, reaching for his glass, grabbing it by the bottom and snatching it out of his reach, "it could be interesting if they were to compare the prints you've left on this glass to the print they lift-ed from the tool they found."

Daria, you gotta love her sometimes, gave a con-vincing performance of a stricken girlfriend.

"Rick, maybe you should — "

"Go ahead," Rick said to me. "Take it. Run along to Daddy and see what he can find out."

"Rick, if the police — "

"Shut up, Daria," he said.

"But if the police — "

"If the police *what?*" Rick said. "They're not going to find anything because there's nothing to find. Get real. Even if I did it, and I'm not saying I did — in fact, I didn't — but even if I did, how stupid do you think I am? You think I'm going to leave my prints all over a metal bar I used to smash in some guy's window?"

Daria glanced at me. She'd caught it too. Who had said anything about a metal bar?

I slid out of the seat, taking the glass with me, holding it gingerly.

"No, I don't think you'd be that stupid, Rick," I said. "You're no Einstein, but you're not an idiot, either. If you weren't wearing gloves when you smashed the window, I'm sure you were smart enough to wipe your fingerprints off the bar before you threw it away."

He looked at the glass and grinned.

"And I'm sure you were also wearing gloves when you photocopied that page from the dictionary, right, Rick?"

His smile wavered like the flame of a candle in a gentle gust of wind.

"Because you know what I just found out, Rick? I just found out that there's this chemical called ninhydrin that the police can use to lift fingerprints off paper. It really works. I also found out that people never think about leaving fingerprints on paper. They wipe their prints off metal and glass and wood. But they hardly ever think about what they're leaving behind on paper. And it just so happens that the cops have the photocopy that was left in Mr. Green's car."

Rick wasn't smiling at all anymore. He slid toward the edge of the bench, then started to lunge toward me. Who knows, he might have caught me, too, if Daria hadn't stuck out her foot and tripped him. He crashed to the floor. I hurried out of Ralph's with the glass.

* * *

The East Hastings *Beacon* was minus one ace high school reporter. The East Hastings Regional High Huskies were minus one ace quarterback, at least temporarily. Rick was suspended from the team because of what he had done to Mr. Green's car. But other than that, life was back to normal. Sort of.

I had history on Tuesday morning. Mr. Green didn't look at me during class. When the bell rang, he asked me to stay behind. I sat where I was until everyone had left. He sat where he was, at his desk. For a few moments, he just stared at me.

Then, with a sigh, he got up.

"I owe you an apology," he said.

"I think you owe me a couple."

He looked startled. The first red splotch appeared just above his collar.

"You accused me of cheating. You accused me of puncturing your tire. And you accused me of breaking into your car. And you didn't have a single piece of solid evidence for any of those things."

His entire neck was red now and his chin was quickly turning crimson.

"You're right," he said. "I'm sorry."

I stared stupidly at him. Not only had he said the words, he had actually sounded sincere.

"Innocent until proven guilty, right?" he said.

I nodded.

"Not a bad thing to keep in mind," he said. Then he actually smiled at me. "You'd better get going," he said, "or you'll be late for your next class." I gathered my books. "Oh, and by the way, your essay on *les filles du roi?*"

I held my breath.

"Excellent work, Chloe," he said. "I gave it an A-plus. And I did that before I knew who really vandalized my car."

I decided to believe him. My turn to smile.

About the Author

Norah McClintock has won five Arthur Ellis Awards for juvenile crime fiction. *The Vancouver Sun* called her a "John Grisham for teens." Her books have been published around the world, and continually receive rave reviews. She lives in Toronto with her family.